Producing Love Together

Musical Curves Series:
Volume Two

By Leanora Cowan

The Musical Curves Series:

-Rhymes From The Heart - Volume One

The Voluptuously Curvy & Loving It Series:

-Smooth As Silk
-Finding Love Within
-His Forgotten Lover
-Drafted For Love
-Planning For Forever

Other Books By Author Leanora Moore:

-The Caress of a Younger Man

-Heavenly Kingdom

What People Are Saying About The Musical Curves Series So Far:

"I truly enjoy your work I have all your book it's nice to read about the plus size women getting love I enjoyed Tazmin and Adonis story can't wait for the next book in this series you keep writing them I'll keep buying them." - **Edna Crapp**

"I won a copy of this book from the author and was very excited to read this book. I fell headfirst into the world of Musical Curves Records with Adonis, Tazmin, and the rest of their families. :-)

Leanora Moore takes you into the world of a highly successful businesswoman - Tazmin - and the trials and tribulations that she experiences while on the journey to her "happily ever after." This book is filled with music, love, family, betrayal, and HEAT ;-) The passion between Tazmin and Adonis sets the pages of the book on fire. This book is well written, and I recommend it to anyone looking for a good love story :-) I look forward to reading the next book in this series." - **Ebony Arrington-McMillan**

"WOW!! Once again Ms. Moore has written a wonderful love story. A page turner for sure. I was so for Adonis to capture the heart of Tazmin. I got a little scared when his big brother was brought in, so

I cheated. lol.... yeah I couldn't take the suspense. Again a great read... worth every dime." – **W. Parks Brigham, Author of, You Were Meant For Me.**

"This book was great...As always Leanora Moore did not disappoint. I cannot wait to read the next book in this series...Please don't keep us waiting long."
  - **Stephanie Williams**

"I loved it. Adonis was just the character that had me in love. Then Tazmin, oh boy. She a sophisticated lady with a good head on her shoulders. I loved it honey!"
  -**Angelique' Teyanna J.**

Acknowledgments

This book is for all my strong and curvy sisters out there that are handling their business in both their personal and professional lives. I wrote this book with each of you in mind, and I want you all to know that there is nothing we can't do as long as we stay focused and fight for it.

I have to thank the love of my life, Justin Cowan. You showed me the type of love I didn't think possible. Soon we will take our vows to begin our life together as husband and wife and I look forward to the years ahead of us - blending our hearts as one.

I would also like to thank my children, Demetrius, Devin, Keonta, Demonte, Demario and Jamal for giving me the courage to keep pushing forward and setting an example that anything is possible.

Producing Love Together

Musical Curves Series:
Volume Two

Chapter One

Feeling soft butterfly kisses being placed down her back, caused Kamala to moan as, she enjoyed the way her lover awakened the flames in her body that had diminished so long ago. Sighing, as she felt his strong hands caressing her butt as if sculpting clay, she couldn't help the moan that had slipped from her mouth. Her nipples hardened and became sensitive as they rubbed against her Egyptian cotton sheets.

With her eyes closed, it seemed as if all her senses were on high alert, as her breath hitched when she felt him leave love bites on her butt going down to her thighs. As he cherished her body, Kamala began to squirm as shockwaves of pleasure started to vibrant toward her core causing her to gasp.

When his warm tongue licked from her thighs up to her butt cheeks, Kamala had to squeeze her eyes tighter as pulses of need hit her womanhood. When she also squeezed her thighs together, she heard him chuckle at her response. Hearing that sexy sound as it seemed to vibrate through her body, Kamala also felt him gently blow on her center as he pried her legs open. His sensual touches only intensified the pressure building in her stomach.

Gripping the sheets as the tension continued to build, and his firm grip on her thighs seemed to set her skin on fire, as she anticipated his next move. Then feeling his masculine fingers massage the delicate folds of her womanhood caused her to suck in a quick breath. The waves of pleasure she was feeling caused Kamala to feel as if she couldn't take anymore, but she didn't dare tell him to stop.

Gasping for air, and grasping the sheets to keep from floating away to oblivion, Kamala soon felt his warm breath on her sensitive folds before she felt his hot tongue touch her
clit.

Squirming on her bed, as he started to attack her sensitive clit, Kamala felt as if she was going to lose touch with reality. The passion flowing through her veins felt like hot lava, as the tension in her stomach tightened even more until her toes felt as if they were curling and she gasped.

Delirious with need, she felt him lightly blow on her clit again before he started to push his fingers slowly into her opening, causing her entire world to explode.

Gasping for air and looking around as she sat up in her bed, Kamala Hardwood realized she was in her hotel suite alone. "What the hell!" she yelled as she ran her hands through her tangled hair.

Taking a deep breath and swinging her legs over the edge of the king size bed, Kamala realized her body was covered in sweat, and her silk nightgown was sticking to her overheated body. Shaking her head, as her heart rate was racing from the erotic dream that had been reoccurring for the past week, with her waking up just as she experienced a mind-blowing orgasm. Taking another deep breath, Kamala tried to remember the mystery guy's face that masterfully manipulated her body into submission.

Standing up on her shaky legs and stretching her tightly wound body, the throbbing between her legs seem to intensify, causing her to gasp. "I seriously have to get laid," she joked as she started to gather her clothes for the day out of her suitcase, just as someone knocked on her door.

Quickly pulling on her robe, and rushing to the door, she opened it to find Demetria, Alondra, Reyna, and Rozlynn standing there along with her other friends Malia Freeman and Livia Caplin. "You look how I feel," Kamala joked as she waved them inside her room.

"Girl, after all the drinking and partying we did last night, I'm surprised I'm up this early," Alondra replied as she sat down on the white sofa between Demetria and Livia.

"Do you have to talk so loudly?" Reyna whispered as she sat down on the other sofa and started to massage her temple causing the group to chuckle.

"We didn't tell you to try and out drink Gunner at the reception last night," Malia joked causing the group to laugh as Reyna rolled her eyes.

The day before, Kamala's best friend, Tazmin Foster married the love of her life, Adonis Elliott. Then the rest of the night, they all had a wonderful time drinking and dancing with Adonis's older brothers Spencer, Liam, and Gunner along with his cousin Rico Elliott.

"For your information, Gunner was trying to keep up with me, and I ended up winning too," Reyna replied as she laid her head back on the sofa with her eyes closed.

"I think we all overdid it last night, but I will say it was well worth it!" Alondra said as she also leaned back into the sofa next to Reyna.

"I bet it was, after the way you and Liam kept flirting all night," Demetria joked causing Alondra to narrow her eyes at her.

"She has a point! I'm surprised that you two didn't finish the deal last night," Kamala added as she sat down in the single white armchair with a smirk on her face.

"I've been telling you guys, that we are just friends. I mean damn, we all grew up together, and I don't even think he sees me like that," Alondra replied before releasing a deep sigh.

"Sis, I hate to be the one to tell you this, and Liam may not have said anything about his interest to you, but you can see it in his eyes whenever you two are together," Rozlynn said as she looked over at Alondra with a smirk on her face.

"Since everyone wants to put me on Front Street, why don't we get Kamala to tell us about her and Desmond? Or Demetria can tell us about her and Spencer?" Alondra replied with a smirk of her own.

"For your information, Desmond and I are just good friends and that's it. He's dating a new flavor of the week," Kamala stated as she recalled how Desmond's new girlfriend, Riley Williams, an interior designer was glued to Desmond's hip the whole week they had been in the Cayman Islands.

"Riley also happens to be the designer helping them remodel the recording studios at their record Label, Musical Curves Records."

"Oh my god! Did you see the dress that chick wore to Tazmin's wedding?" Malia yelled.

"Shit, everybody saw that small piece of cloth she called a dress. I was praying she didn't take a deep breath because she would have given everyone a view of her goodies," Livia replied laughing.

"I had to stop Tazmin from cussing her out, for showing up like that," Kamala said smiling.

"Desmond could do so much better! Yes, the woman is a great interior designer, but she needs a fashion consultant badly," Rozlynn stated.

Listening to the conversation, Kamala couldn't understand why it bothered her so much that Desmond had brought another woman to the Grand Cayman Islands for Tazmin and Adonis's wedding since they were just friends.

"To be honest, I think Desmond, Spencer, Liam, and Gunner could do better than the women they brought on this trip. Who knows what could happen in the future," Malia stated smiling.

Kamala just rolled her eyes and shook her head. "On that statement, I'm going to suggest we go get something to eat before we continue this topic.

"That chick with Liam almost got the hell knocked out of her last night," Reyna stated as she sat on the edge of her seat.

"I agree! Plus I'm starving, and I want to hear all the juicy details," Livia added causing the group to laugh.

"Alright, let me go throw on some clothes, and I'll be ready," Kamala agreed as she stood up and then headed to her bedroom.

Entering the bedroom, Kamala couldn't stop thinking about how good Desmond looked in his tuxedo the night before. How good it felt to be in his arms as they danced a few songs together, that is until the flavor of the week cut in. Putting on her water-colored maxi dress that had an empire waistband, Kamala knew that she needed to finally end the crush she had on Desmond. He would rather be with a woman who wore a size six instead of a woman who wore a size twenty-four.

Taking a deep breath as she finished getting dressed and applying a little makeup, Kamala pushed all those insecurities to the back of her mind. She decided to enjoy her vacation and hoped that she would meet a good-looking island man to take her mind off of Desmond.

Chapter Two

"I need a man!" Kamala thought as she sat in her office two weeks later. She was trying to get ready for her next meeting with the Vice-Presidents of the Label, but all she could think about was the erotic dreams that kept reoccurring each night. After being home two weeks since the wedding, those dreams were becoming more intense, and her body and hormones are going crazy. Every morning she would wake up feeling like she had just run a marathon, gasping for air and her heart racing.

Then to make matters worse, she still couldn't figure out who the guy was that was sexing her so good until her toes curled. She was screaming as her body felt as if it could explode into a million pieces. She could see the outline of his muscled body in the dimly lit room, but no matter how hard she tried, she couldn't make out his face. Sighing, Kamala stood up and started collecting the paperwork that she needed for the meeting.

As the Senior Vice-President of the Label and with Tazmin, who was the president, gone on her honeymoon for two weeks, Kamala was in charge and had to keep everyone on track. Walking out of her office and onto the elevator, she thought about Tazmin and Adonis, and how they proved that true love was worth fighting for. Their relationship started when Adonis was signed to the Label, and over the next few months they fell in love. Even though they had a lot of drama with Adonis's ex-girlfriend popping up and starting problems, and with the media all in their business, they still loved each other and got married. Most importantly, they were also expecting their first child in a couple of months.

Kamala was so happy for her friends because Tazmin had always taken care of her siblings when their parents were murdered. That's when she became an instant parent to her four younger sisters and not once did she complain. Then Adonis entered the picture, and it was finally her time to find love and happiness.

Walking off the elevator, she was greeted by the sisters, Demetria, and Alondra Foster, who were talking and laughing together.

"What's so funny?" Kamala asked as she hugged her friends.

"Alondra was telling me about her date last night with Easton Shaw, the new point guard for the Chicago Bulls," Demetria replied, causing Alondra to roll her eyes.

"I want to hear this!" Kamala said smiling as she recalled how fine Easton was at six foot six inches tall with brown eyes and a toned body.

"To be honest, I had a wonderful time, and we do have a lot in common. He even tried to teach me how to bowl, and even when I kept rolling the ball into the gutter, he tried to make me feel better," Alondra replied smiling.

"That's a brave brother because the last time we all went bowling, you tried to slide down the lane with the ball still in your hand," Demetria joked. Kamala laughed as she remembered that incident too.

"Very funny you two," Alondra replied as she rolled her eyes again.

Looking down at her diamond Rolex watch, "Guys, let's start the meeting, and at dinner tonight I want to hear the rest of this adventurous date," Kamala joked as she put her arm around Alondra and smiled.

"Yes, let's get started and I'll think about telling you guys about my date since you both have jokes," Alondra replied. Then they turned around and walked into the boardroom, where everyone was already seated.

"Hello everyone!" Kamala greeted as she took her seat at the head of the table. "As everyone knows, Tazmin will be gone for two more weeks, so we all have to chip in and keep pushing forward. So let's start by talking about our current clients and what needs to be done for them to be successful," Kamala continued as she looked around the table.

Reyna Foster, who was the Vice-President of Artist and Repertoire Department, added, "I'll start. Jasmine is currently getting ready to release her new album along with Cyrus,"

Jasmine Kelly was their R&B diva, who had been signed to their Label two years before. Cyrus Baldwin was signed to the Label around the same time as Adonis and had been burning up the R&B music charts.

Cheyenne Reggie, who was Vice-President of the Public Relations Department added, "We have also scheduled interviews for the both of them as well as finalized the itinerary for their upcoming tours."

"Alright, what about Godric? How is his new album coming along?" Kamala asked as her eyes panned the table.

Godric Dawson was a veteran in the music game and had been signed to the Label to revamp his career. Since he had joined the Label, his music had earned him numerous awards.

"His album is almost finished. I talked with him and Desmond, and Desmond said he just needed to put his finishing touches on it," Reyna replied.

Hearing Desmond's name caused Kamala's breath to hitch and her heart to race. Her inner voice questioned this reaction to the man she merely considered a friend.

Shaking her head, she said aloud, "Alright let's move on to our new artist. What's going on with Grayson Banner and Carter Dixon?" Kamala asked before taking a deep breath to calm the butterflies fluttering in her stomach.

"They both have started their first major album with Desmond, and from what I've heard so far, they are both going to take over the R&B charts," Reyna replied.

"We have also started working on their promotional planning because both of them have a sex appeal that will draw women to them like crazy," Malia Freeman added, who was Vice-President of Promotions.

"We have also set up interviews with Essence, Entertainment Weekly, Vibe, and Source magazine for both artists. Plus interviews with major radio stations and TV shows," Cheyenne added.

Rozlynn Foster, Vice-President of Artist Development added, "We also set them up with media coaching and a fashion stylist."

"My team is already brainstorming a marketing plan for each of their albums, and we will coordinate with the other departments, as usual," Livia Caplin, the Vice-President of the Marketing Department added.

"As far as their internet presence, they both have a huge following on social media.
So my team will help in those areas too, and once their music videos are done, we will start promoting them also,"

Jenelle Wilson, Vice-President of the New Media Department, stated.

"It sounds like we are on track. And when Tazmin and Adonis come back from their honeymoon, he'll finish his new album. So start brainstorming for his promotional plan. Alondra and Demetria, how are the legal matters with Godric going regarding the whole tax issues with the IRS?" Kamala asked.

"I was able to meet with Godric and the tax auditor to straighten out his tax issues. I also found him a new personal accountant, who is a close friend of mine," replied Alondra who was Vice-President of Business Affairs.

Demetria who was Vice-President of the Legal Department added, "On my end, I helped him file a civil case against his former accountant, who was stealing from him. So now everything is straightened out, and he can focus on producing great music."

"Well guys, it seems that everyone is on track. So keep doing what you're doing, and we will meet again next week," Kamala said as she stood up, and then everyone followed her lead.

"Are we still on for dinner at Gibson's tonight?" Reyna asked as she gathered her papers and electronic tablet.

"Of course. Plus, I need a strong margarita," Kamala joked causing the ladies to chuckle as they followed her out of the boardroom. "I'll meet you guys there at six," she continued as she pressed the up button on the elevator.

"See you there," the other ladies replied as they walked toward their offices.

Stepping onto the elevator, Kamala leaned back against the elevator wall. While taking a deep breath, she realized with Tazmin being gone for two more weeks, her work week was going to be terribly busy. A drink with the girls was the only thing keeping her from pulling her hair out.

Ending a conference call, Kamala leaned back in her leather office chair and closed her eyes as she felt a migraine starting. All that day she had been on calls with suppliers and local officials building new industry relationships for the Label.

Kamala loved her career and wouldn't change it for anything. She made more money than she would ever spend, and she enjoyed helping their artists develop great music, and most of all she enjoyed doing it with her family.

Since her father, Luke Hardwood, had left her and her mother, Sophia Hardwood, Kamala had a tough time trusting people. It was then that she met Tazmin at Freshman orientation at the University of Chicago. Once they realized they were roommates, they became close friends. After getting to know Tazmin and her family. She came to love them as her very own family. She was there for Tazmin as she raised her four siblings, after their parents died. Kamala had developed a profound respect for Tazmin and her family. Then during her senior year in college, her own mother suddenly passed away, from a brain aneurysm, causing Kamala to feel so alone.

It was then that Tazmin, and her family along with Desmond Fleming, who also attended the same college, stepped in and offered her their love and support. Desmond was a close friend, who didn't mind stepping in, giving her a shoulder to lean on as needed during the hardest part of her grief.

Just thinking about her mother brought tears to her eyes. Even though her mother was always working two jobs, she did what she could to make time for Kamala when she needed her.

"Kamala, are you alright?" She froze. That voice always sent a shiver down her spine and getting her heart rate racing. But it couldn't be him, she thought as she squeezed her eyes shut.

Opening her eyes and wiping her cheek, she looked into his beautiful brown eyes and saw his concern for her. Taking a deep breath as she let her eyes scan his black dress slacks, and a navy polo shirt that showed his muscular arms perfectly.

Clearing her throat, she murmured, "I'm f-fine, just thinking about my mom." Grabbing a tissue out of the box on her desk, she watched as he sat down in one of the white leather chairs in front of her desk.

"Do you need anything?" he asked as he leaned back in his chair causing her breath to hitch as his chest muscles flexed under his shirt.

"No, I'm fine!" she assured him before smiling. She narrowed her eyes at him. "So what do I owe for the honor of this visit?" she asked as she placed her arms on her desk and leaned forward.

"Well I had to come and check on you since I haven't seen you since the wedding," he stated smiling.

"That's so sweet of you! I have been so busy since I've been back, and you've been busy finishing everyone's albums. It's no wonder we haven't seen each other," Kamala stated as she leaned back in her chair.

"You are right, we have been busy. But we have always made time to check in with each other," Desmond replied with his signature smile and cute dimples.

"Well, now that you are dating Ms. Williams, I figured you had your hands full," she stated before she could stop herself.

Kamala didn't know what possessed her to say that, and she wished the floor would open up and swallow her.

"Come on Kamala, you know that you are one of my closest friends and nothing, or no one is going to change that. Why would you think otherwise?" he asked as his eyes probed hers causing her heart to accelerate.

Taking a deep breath she said, "Desmond, I was just joking. You are one of my closest friends also, and I understand that you have a busy life," Lifting her hand to move her hair from her eyes, she continued. "I mean If dating Ms. Williams makes you happy, then I'm happy for you," she insisted, wondering if she was trying to convince him or herself.

"It's cool! Just know that I'm always here for you no matter what."

"I know," she stated just as his cell phone chimed.

"Damn, I forgot I'm meeting Riley for lunch," Desmond mumbled as his fingers tapped a quick text. Kamala felt an instant thrum of irritation and disappointment.

"Desmond it's alright, go and enjoy your lunch, and we can catch up later," Kamala said with a little more bite than she intended. Biting her lip to keep from saying anything further she diverted her attention to the files she needed for her next meeting.

Standing up and looking down at her, he waited until her gaze met his. "Thanks for understanding. And let's get together for lunch this week, okay?" His mouth eased into the smile that did crazy things to her insides.

"Let me know when and where," she said smiling.

"I'll call you later," he replied as he started walking towards the door just as his phone went off again.

"All right!" she said just before he walked out of the door.

When the door closed, Kamala sighed and leaned back in her chair as she realized that while she was pining over Desmond, he was continuing to date. Plus, he hadn't shown that he had any romantic feelings for her in all the years they had known each other. Turning around in her chair to look at Chicago's skyline out of her window, Kamala also realized it was time for a change, and she needed to find her happiness and possible love.

Chapter Three

Sitting at his table in Spiaggia on North Michigan Avenue, Desmond Fleming was so confused and didn't know how to fix the issues in his personal life. As he was waiting for his girlfriend to arrive for lunch, he couldn't help thinking about the conversation he had with Kamala. He could see the sadness in her eyes that she had tried to cover up with a fake smile and jokes.

He and Kamala had been close friends since college, and he still remembered the day he met her as if it were yesterday. He was in the freshman orientation and his roommate Justin Freeman decided to flirt with these two fine sisters that were there also. Both ladies had bodies that would make any man say amen, and their smiles seemed to light up the room. So being a good wingman for Justin, they both decided to approach the ladies. Desmond had to chuckle as he remembered how Tazmin and Kamala both told Justin they had boyfriends. It was funny the way his smile fell from his face as if he had just lost his favorite toy.

Even though they both had boyfriends, they all had become close friends, even though Desmond had a crush on the both of them. As years passed by, his crush on Tazmin changed to the same feeling he had toward his sister. When it came to Kamala, he was still confused about his feelings for her and didn't know what to do about them. She meant more to him than just a close friend, but he couldn't for the life of him define those feelings.

When they spoke earlier, she had brought up him dating Riley, and he didn't know if it was just him or not, but he thought she seemed a little jealous. Shaking his head, Desmond knew that there was no way Kamala would be jealous of his relationship when she could have any man she wanted. Looking around the restaurant, he couldn't stop feeling as if he had been neglecting their friendship to be with Riley. Never would he want to hurt Kamala, and he knew that he had to make it up to her somehow.

"Hello handsome," a female voice said behind him before she kissed his cheek.

Looking up, Desmond saw Riley looking as beautiful as ever wearing a red dress that left little to the imagination. He frowned.

"Hello beautiful," he replied as he stood up and hugged her, before assisting her with her chair and then returning to his own.

"Sorry I'm so late, I had an emergency situation at one of my client's homes," Riley said smiling.

"It's alright, I haven't been here that long myself. So what was this emergency?" he asked as their waiter arrived.

"Hello, I'm Larry, and I'll be your server today! What would you like to drink and have as appetizers for starters?" Larry asked as he handed them their menus.

"I'll have an iced tea with lemon," Riley replied as she continued to look at her menu.

"I'll have the same," Desmond added as he couldn't shake the nagging feeling that he forgot something important.

"I'll be right back with your drinks," Larry replied before walking away.

Looking over at Riley, Desmond thought about when they had first met when she started remodeling the studios at the Label, and her laugh and smile drew him in like a moth to a flame. Not to mention, she had a body to die for. But looking at her now, it suddenly felt as if something were missing, and he just couldn't figure out what it was. She was smart, successful, and beautiful so what more could he want?

"Baby, what are you having?" Riley asked as she looked over at him, smiling.

"I'm not very hungry, so I'll have the Fegliatelle Nere," Desmond replied, which was jumbo lump crab, Calabrian pepper, and pasta with red onions.

Hearing her endearment for him, for some reason didn't sound right coming from her lips, and he had to quickly cover up the frown on his face when her smile started to fall.

"Desmond, what's wrong? You seem out of it today," she asked as she laid her hand over his, across the table.

Clearing his throat, "I'm fine, I just have a lot on my mind," he replied as Larry walked up to the table with their drinks.

"Here are your drinks, are you ready to order your entrees?" he asked. He placed their drinks on the table, but suddenly Desmond had lost his appetite as his cell phone started to ring.

His eyes met Riley's and found her glance from him to the phone he pulled from his pocket. Seeing Kamala's name on his caller ID instantly brought a smile to his face.

"Hello!" He looked over at Riley again and dropped the goofy smile that was on his face.

"Hello, I'm sorry to call you, but Godric just called me and asked where you were. You two were supposed to meet at the studio at one o'clock, and now it's two o'clock," Kamala replied causing Desmond to groan.

"Damn! Tell him I'll be there as soon as possible," Desmond stated as he stood up and grabbed his jacket off of his chair.

"I'll let him know," Kamala said before ending the call.

Looking down at Riley he placed his hand gently on her shoulder, "I'm sorry, but I need to head back to the studio,"

"Is everything alright?" Her eyes were full of concern as they looked up at him.

"Yeah, I just forgot about a meeting with Godric. I can't believe that slipped my mind. We're supposed to be putting the final touches on his album. Babe, I promise I'll make it up to you." he stated as he leaned down and kissed her forehead. "Here's my credit card. That should take care of everything. I'll call you later," he replied before he rushed away from her toward the front of the restaurant. Then she looked across the restaurant and captured the eye of the server. He quickly walked over.

"How may I help you, Madame?"

"I'll take the check. My friend had an emergency and I've lost my appetite."

"Understood, Madame. It'll just be a moment." He soon came back with the leather folder holding the receipt, which she signed with a flourish before reaching in her purse and placing cash on top." Then she zipped Desmond's credit card inside her wallet that she dropped inside her designer purse.

Stepping into the night relieved her more than she could ever have imagined. Catching sight of Desmond's car as it pulled off brought forth a discontent sigh releasing questions rising within.

Desmond slipped a bill in the valet's hand and quickly slid inside his new Cadillac Escalade mere moments after the valet had arrived in front of the restaurant. Taking a deep breath as he shook his head, Desmond headed to the Label. He couldn't believe he forgot something that important, especially when they were trying to finish Godric's album as soon as possible.

Desmond knew he needed to relax. He couldn't help but think that Kamala may have had a point about him neglecting everything because he was dating Riley. Normally he wouldn't have ever forgotten a recording session and even his family had said the same thing to him, but he had brushed it off.

Leaning back into the custom leather seats, he couldn't get Kamala's sensual voice out of his mind. He also couldn't help but compare Kamala and Riley, since they both had bodies of a goddess and smiles that lit up a room. Kamala vibed with him on an intellectual level, and they had so much in common. Shaking his head as he pulled up in front of the Label Desmond knew that he and Kamala were only going to be friends, and he needed to focus on his relationship with Riley.

Walking into the building, Desmond didn't know what he was going to do, but he knew he needed to make some important decisions soon before someone ended up getting hurt.

Chapter Four

The next day as she rode the elevator to the ninth floor, Kamala looked at herself in the gleaming elevator doors. She realized that her new red pencil skirt dress with chic cap-sleeves and asymmetrical design on the lined bodice was hugging her voluptuous curves perfectly. The skinny black belt and black accessories completed her look. Her hair fell around her shoulders in soft curls. Turning to the side, she realized her sexy black strappy heels added more sexiness to her look.

Arriving at her floor with a little pep in her step, Kamala headed toward the new and improved studio, and she had to keep taking deep breaths as her heartrate started to race. Knowing she was about to meet with Desmond, she knew she had to play it cool. Once she reached the studio door, she took another deep breath before pushing the door open. When she walked into the room, she was blown away by the fresh look of the studio.

"Do you like it?" There was only one voice that sounded like that and it brought a smile to her face as she looked over at Desmond. He was sitting in front of the soundboard, dressed in blue jeans and a red polo shirt looking sexy as hell.

Clearing her suddenly dry throat she replied. "It looks amazing! Ms. Williams did an excellent job."

Kamala's eyes flitted around at the white leather sofas, white office chairs, the state-of-the-art soundboard, and monitors, then to the purple walls and ceilings complimented by the new light fixtures. Not one detail was spared right down to the luxurious surround sound speakers and new sound booth.

"Yeah, she did a great job decorating all three studios, now I can get back to work. I need to get the final touches done on Godric's album," Desmond said as Kamala sat down in the office chair beside him.

"You look like you could use a break, what's going on with you?" Kamala asked as she looked into his eyes. It was evident that he had a lot on his mind.

He inhaled deeply. "It's nothing, I just have a lot of stuff going on and only a little time to get it done," he replied while he leaned back in his chair and closed his eyes.

"Is this about your workload or is it personal?" she asked. She dreaded his answer because she really didn't want to hear about him and Riley's relationship.

Opening his eyes he looked over at her, "It's both. But staying in the studio is the only time I can relax while I focus on making music," he replied.

"Desmond, I'm here if you ever need to talk. If you need more time on your projects, just let us know," she said as she covered his hand with hers and savored the warmth coming from his skin.

Looking into her eyes and intertwining their fingers together, "I appreciate that, and I will keep that in mind. Now tell me what brings you to my neck of the woods?" he asked, causing her breath to hitch ever so slightly.

Clearing her throat, "I came to check out the studio and to see how Godric's project was coming along," she replied as she pulled her hand back and then leaned away in her chair.

"Besides finishing Godric's album, I'm also working on beats for Adonis' new album. So when he and Tazmin get back, it will be ready," Desmond stated. Kamala's eyes flit over his sexy face down to his muscular chest outlined in his shirt.

"That's good to hear! If everything goes well tonight, I may have a new artist for you to start working with very soon," Kamala said as she started running her hand over the new dials on the soundboard.

"Is that so? Who is this new artist?" he asked causing her to look over at him as he leaned forward in his chair smiling.

"Since it's Friday, the girls and I are going to Club Heat to check out this popular rapper called Malik," she revealed, smiling as Desmond's smile seemed to brighten.

"You have got to be kidding me! That kid has a huge following on social media, and his YouTube videos are amazing," he replied.   "We know, that's why we are going to check him out. Plus, Sonny invited us to the club for his birthday celebration," Kamala said smiling as she noticed his nostrils flare at the mention of Sonny Curtis.

Sonny Curtis was a close friend of theirs, and he had a bad habit of flirting with anything breathing, and he also had a huge crush on Tazmin.

"Please don't mention that fool's name," Desmond stated as he leaned back in his chair again with eyes closed.

"You need to stop holding that grudge against Sonny. It was five years ago, and Sonny knows to never try to push up on me or Tazmin anymore after you, John, and Lance got through with him," she replied. She remembered that night when they all had gone out for drinks, and Sonny had too much to drink and then kept harassing her and Tazmin. Desmond punched him in his jaw, and Tazmin's security, John Avery and Lance Jenkins escorted Sonny out of the club.

"Whatever! I don't like the dude and that's not going to change. As for Malik, I can't wait to work with him," Desmond said as he looked down at his watch.

"That's my cue to let you get back to work. Don't forget what I said about if you need more time," she said as she stood up and smiled at him.

Standing up also, "You don't have to leave. Godric will be here in an hour or so," Desmond replied as his eyes probed into hers as if he were searching for something she may have been hiding.

"It's alright! I need to get back to my office and work on all that paperwork that's piling up on my desk," she said as she touched his arm. She could have sworn that she felt his muscles flex beneath her hand before she drew back her hand.

"Well, I'll see you later, and you ladies try to stay out of trouble tonight," he joked smirking.

"I can't make any promises," Kamala said while walking to the studio door. Glancing over her shoulder one last time, she found him looking at her butt. She cleared her throat, drawing his eyes up to hers.

Licking his juicy lips he shrugged, "Hey you can't blame a guy for looking."

Suddenly envisioning herself clad in only her lacy peach bra and throng beneath his perusal, she said aloud, "Let me get going before you start something that you can't finish." With that, she reached for the doorknob.

Desmond threw his hands up. "Hey! I'm just speaking the truth, but you can run if you want," he joked causing her to roll her eyes as they both started laughing. Then she walked out of the room still shaking her head.

Walking down the hallway headed to the elevator, Kamala didn't know how much more of their joking and flirting she could take before she ended up losing her mind.

Sitting in Mike Ditka's Chicago restaurant, with Demetria, Reyna, Alondra, and Rozlynn while sipping on her Passion Play martini, Kamala longed for a drink after meeting with Desmond.

"What's going on with you, Kamala?" Reyna asked before sipping her martini.

"Nothing much, just work as usual. You are the one who went on the date last night with Russell Jackson, so how did it go?" Kamala deflected causing everyone to focus on Reyna which resulted in an immediate roll of her friend's eyes.

"If you must know, it was a disaster! He had no sense of humor and only talked about himself and his new car," Reyna whined, frowning.

"I don't understand what's going on with these guys these days! It's like they think all women are gold diggers, so they brag about their money and houses like idiots," Alondra sympathized before sipping her drink.

"It's funny you should say that because I read an article today in *Cosmo* that talked about today's dating world. Out of a hundred women, ninety percent said that if a man bragged about his money that it's a major turn-off," Demetria added shaking her head.

"You would think guys would have gotten the memo that we need more than expensive gifts," Reyna added.

"Girl, you are preaching to the choir! The dating scene is so bad, I'm thinking about becoming a nun," Kamala joked, causing the group to chuckle.

"I feel you! The last few dates I've been on weren't even worth me going through the trouble of getting all dressed up," Rozlynn said before turning up the last of her drink.

"Something's got to change because I do want to find love and happiness. After seeing Tazmin and Adonis together, I know it's possible," Kamala stated before finishing her drink, just as their waiter walked up to their table with another round.

"I agree! I say we toast to finding love and happiness," Demetria suggested as she raised her glass, and the rest of the group followed her lead.

As the ladies continued to talk, Kamala couldn't help wondering if Desmond was the key to her happy ending or was she just wasting time thinking he was the one.

Chapter Five

Desmond inhaled deeply after watching Kamala walk out of the studio. Reclaiming his seat he allowed his foot to turn him a bit as he searched through his reaction every time she was near him. Just being around her had his blood rushing to surprising places. Seeing her curvy body in that red dress only revved up his imagination.

Running a hand over his face, Desmond knew that his attraction for Kamala was getting stronger, and he had to do something before he lost his damn mind. Even though his body was telling him to act on his physical needs, his mind was reminding him that Kamala may not feel the same way, and he didn't want to lose a close friend.

Since they met in college, he, Kamala, and Tazmin had been the three amigos and had vowed to set the music industry on fire. So they all studied hard and became each other's support system.

In the years since meeting Kamala, she had been there for him when he needed her the most and not once had she complained. Through the loss of his parents, Desmond was able to see who his loyal friends were.

Kamala had stayed by his side and offered words of encouragement. Her kind heart and generosity were what drew him to her even more. She had even nursed him back to health when he had the flu and was acting like a five-year-old. That was the moment that had opened his eyes to his true feelings for Kamala. That was the moment he realized she was the kind of woman that he needed in his life.

Sighing and laying his head back on the chair with his eyes closed, Desmond could easily picture Kamala with her bright smile and twinkling eyes. Then when he tried to picture Riley, all he could see was a blurred picture. Shaking his head, he tried to focus on his up-and-coming projects and then he thought about Adonis and his new album. Which then caused him to think about Adonis and Tazmin's wedding, and how beautiful Kamala looked as she walk down the aisle as the maid of honor. Her smile drew him in, and that strapless dress held his attention the rest of the night.

Leaning forward and putting his arms on the edge of the soundboard, Desmond thought about the advice Conrad Arnold had given him. Conrad was Adonis' manager and he had given him and Adonis his words of wisdom when they both were confused about what to do with their romantic lives. Conrad had suggested that they both get up the nerve to tell Tazmin and Kamala about their feelings for them. The only one to listen to that advice was Adonis, which ended with him and Tazmin getting married, and they were expecting their first child shortly.

"How did my life become so damn confusing?" he yelled as he fell back in his chair.

"Maybe your older sister can help?" a female voice replied causing a smile to come to his face as he looked over at his sister, Kingsley Lewis.

"I doubt it, but what brings you to my neck of the woods?" he asked standing up before they hugged.

"Can't I just stop by and check on you, since I haven't seen you in weeks?" she asked as they both sat down in the two office chairs facing each other.

Smiling, "You act like it's been months since we've talked. Plus, you know that I went to Tazmin and Adonis's wedding, and then when I got back, I had to catch up on my work," he stated.

Looking at his sister, who was two years older than him. At thirty-seven, she reminded him a lot of his mother with her smooth pecan brown skin and vibrant Hershey chocolate eyes. Kingsley had the fashion sense of a designer, always wearing the latest fashion trends along with a fresh pixie haircut. As a plus-sized woman, even as a teacher for third graders, she felt she should always look her best.

"Desmond, do you realize it's been three weeks since I've heard from you. Then I hear that you, Adam, and Ryder are getting together for a guy's night tonight, but I couldn't even get a kiss my ass or nothing from you?" she asked as her eyes narrowed at him.

Desmond paused as he thought about the time frame for the past month and was shocked at his behavior.

He sighed. "Sis, I'm so sorry, but with the wedding and work, I've been very busy," he replied before running his hand through his dreads that fell past his shoulders.

"I understand you're a busy man, but since you started seeing this new chick, it's like you don't think about anything else. I want you to be happy, but I just don't see that happening with her," Kingsley stated as she leaned forward in her chair.

"To keep it one hundred, I don't see us dating much longer. Riley is a great woman, but we don't vibe enough to make a relationship last," Desmond replied, feeling an inexplainable relief on saying it aloud.

"Bro, I can't tell you how to run your life. I will say that when you meet the right woman, you will know it," she stated as she patted his hand that was on the armrest of his chair.

"I hope you're right! Now enough about my life, what's going on with you?" he asked smiling.

"Well since you asked, Adam and I just found out we are two months pregnant!" she yelled causing Desmond to jump up and pull her into his arms as they hugged.

"Congratulations, Sis! So I'm finally going to be an uncle?" he asked as they pulled apart smiling at each other.

"Yes, you are! We told Ryder this past Sunday at the family dinner, so now everyone knows," she replied.

Desmond remembered her earlier statement, and he realized he had been missing their family dinners to be with Riley because she always complained about wanting them to spend time alone. Maybe Kamala and Kingsley had a point about him focusing on Riley too much.

"I'm sorry I wasn't there, but I promise to be there this Sunday," he said smiling.

"You better be there! I'm making my famous lasagna and for dessert I'm making your favorite, German chocolate cake," she stated causing him to close his eyes and groan, which caused her to laugh.

"You know I never miss your lasagna, plus I've missed you guys," he said as he leaned forward in his chair.

"We missed you too, and since you are coming, I'll make sure Adam and Ryder don't touch the food until you get there," Kingsley joked as she stood up, smiling.

"I would love to see their faces when you tell them to wait," he replied causing her to chuckle.

"Ha! Well I need to head back to work, but I will see you Sunday," she said as she hugged him.

"I'll be there, and you drive carefully, especially now that you are carrying my niece or nephew," he joked as they pulled apart.

"Will do, and I love you," she replied as she walked toward the door.

"Love you too," he stated just before she walked out of the studio.

Seeing the door close behind Kingsley, Desmond returned to his seat with a smile on his face as he realized his family was about to become bigger. He was so happy for sister and brother-in-law. They had been trying to have a child since they were married six years ago, and after visiting numerous doctors, they finally got their miracle baby. Thinking about how happy Kingsley and Adam were together, Desmond realized he wanted that for himself. He was ready to make some changes.

Later that night riding in the back of her new Rolls Royce Ghost, Kamala was headed to Club Heat to meet up with the girls. She looked down at her black off-the-shoulder sequined dress that had a draped bodice and empire waist. With its just-below-the-knee flared skirt, she felt sexy, and she knew her toned legs looked great since she was also wearing her favorite black strappy heels. To finish her look, she had the matching clutch purse with metallic accents.

She looked in the front seat to see her bodyguards, Nicole Kennedy, and Kevin Jacob talking as usual. Watching them, she wondered if they had finally admitted their feelings for each other. They both had admitted it to her, but as far as she knew they still hadn't told each other.

Watching them laugh and talk, she was reminded of Tazmin and Adonis, and how their world wind romance had started. When Adonis had joined the Label, everyone could see his interest in Tazmin, but Tazmin.

Kamala could understand why though, because like herself, Tazmin's career was very demanding, and with past hurts and disappointments, Tazmin had decided to shut romance out of her life.

Then in walks Adonis, who broke down all the walls around Tazmin's heart and showed her what true love was. Through all the odds and their busy careers, they had gotten married and had a child on the way.

Looking out the window as they cruised down North Halsted Street, Kamala realized she had achieved getting an excellent education, graduating with honors. She had a successful career with the largest and hottest Label in the music industry, and yet her life felt as if it was missing something. Sure she had been on many dates, and even though none of them had worked out, she had gained some great friends.

Kamala realized she needed and wanted her own happily-ever-after, and she couldn't sit back and put her life on hold because of a crush she had on Desmond.

When they pulled up to the club, Kamala felt a rush of excitement as she looked at the line of people, dressed to impress and waiting to get into the popular nightclub. When Kevin opened her door and offered her his hand, Kamala could hear the booming music coming from inside the club, and it set off a current of adrenaline within her.

She couldn't wait to start ladies' night with the girls. Stepping out of the car, with Nicole on one side of her and Kevin on the other side, Kamala was instantly blinded by the flashes of cameras and people screaming her name. Smiling and waving at everyone, Kamala was led into the club and was greeted by the packed house of people having a good time mingling and getting their drink on. Her eyes slid across the people on the dance floor shaking what their mama gave them.

"This club is bumping tonight," Kevin yelled as he led her through the club.

"I know! Everyone is celebrating Sonny's birthday and came to see this new rapper called Malik perform," Kamala yelled back as she waved at members of the media.

"They are in for a treat then because I caught one of Malik's shows at Club Rolex, and they almost brought the club down. He was so entertaining," Nicole said as they headed to the VIP area. She could see that her group had already arrived.

"That's good to know since we may be signing him," Kamala said as she bobbed her head to the music playing.

"I'm not surprised, he's going to be a huge star," Kevin said just as they reached the VIP area.

"We will be nearby. So enjoy yourself," Nicole said before Kamala stepped past the velvet ropes that separated the area.

"Alright guys," she replied as she smiled at them, and then walked over to her group.

"It's about time!" Demetria said as she stood up and hugged Kamala.

"I left the office later than I planned, but I'm here now. So let's get our drink on," Kamala said as she hugged the rest of the group and then sat down on the white lounge sofa between Demetria and Reyna.

Looking around the group, Kamala could see that the ladies had come dressed to impress. As plus-sized women, they each had a unique fashion sense and loved the latest trends, resulting from many shopping trips.

"Don't feel bad, I just got here too. I had to finish looking over the proofs for Jasmine's promotional materials before I left for the day," Saige Archer, the art department V.P., added.

"Since we all had a busy day, I think it calls for a night of drinking and dancing," Alondra stated just as their waiter walked up and handed each of the ladies an Appletini.

"I agree and for the rest of the night, we focus on having a fun time. While Reyna focuses on signing our next big star," Kamala added as she raised her glass and clinked it against other ladies' glasses.

"Well if it isn't my favorite group of ladies," Sonny greeted as he walked into their area, causing the ladies to smile.

Sonny was the best example of a fine and successful man, with him owning numerous clubs on the east coast and having a bodybuilder's physique.

Well, if it isn't the birthday boy! Happy Birthday Sonny," Kamala greeted as she stood up and hugged him.

"Thank you! Are you ladies having fun tonight?" he asked as he hugged the rest of the group.

"You know we always enjoy ourselves when we come here and thank you for inviting us up to your party," Demetria replied after she hugged him.

"I aim to please! You ladies let me know if you need anything, and your drinks are on the house," Sonny added as he glanced around the group.

"Thank you, Sonny, and you enjoy your night also," Kamala added as she raised her glass up at him smiling.

"I will if you promise to save me a dance later," Sonny replied smiling.

Kamala shook her head as she smiled at his weak attempt to flirt with her, despite knowing that he was in love with Tazmin.

"That can be arranged since it is your birthday," Kamala replied before she saw his smile blossom.

"Thank you, and I also want a dance from the rest of you also," he added as he then looked around the group.

"Anything for you Sonny," Reyna replied as she raised her glass up at him also.

"Well now that I know that I get to share my evening with the finest women in the club, I can go get this party started," Sonny stated causing Kamala to shake her head before taking a sip of her drink.

"We can't wait to see the artists you have performing tonight," Rozlynn said before sipping some of her drink.

"Well, you are in for a major surprise, then! Let me go introduce the first artist of the night and I will see you ladies later," Sonny said as he winked at Kamala.

"You are a hot mess!" Kamala joked causing the group to chuckle.

"Hey, what can I say? Being around you all, has hypnotized me," he replied before he walked away causing the group to laugh. "That man is as crazy as they come, but he is a genius when it comes to business," Alondra stated before finishing her drink and signaling their waiter.

"You do have a point there and having this big showcase for this party is drawing in some serious revenue," Malia added as their waiter arrived and started refilling everyone's glasses.

"I can't wait to see Malik perform again. He has the body of a God and the voice to make any woman's knees weak," Aleisha Gale V.P. of the Record Label's Liaison Department stated before taking a sip of her drink.

"I'm with you Aleisha," Cheyenne added as she high-fived, Aleisha.

"You two are crazy! I can't wait to see what all the hype is about," Kamala said as she looked around the club. Then she came eye to eye with someone from her past that she hadn't seen since high school, Dominic Taylor.

"What in the hell?" she said causing the group to look at her.

"What's wrong Kamala?" Demetria asked as Kamala watched Dominic walk across the club toward her.

Clearing her throat, "One of my ex-boyfriends from high school is headed this way. He's the one dressed in the black shirt and dress slacks with the gray silk tie," she replied as she took in his muscular physique and handsome smile with his kissable dimples.

"Damned, if you don't want him, I'll take him," Malia joked causing Kamala to smile.

Malia was currently engaged to Dexter Rogers, who was a highly successful basketball player.

The closer he came, Kamala had to remind herself to breathe. When he arrived at the entrance of the VIP area, Kevin and Nicole quickly stopped him and caused Kamala to stand up and walk over to them.

"Guys it's alright, I know him," Kamala stated as she stood between Kevin and Nicole as she looked up at Dominic while he smiled down at her.

"Alright, let us know if you need anything," Nicole replied before she and Kevin stepped back to their post.

"Well, if it isn't the lovely Kamala Hardwood," Dominic greeted smiling.

"And if it isn't Mr. MVP, Dominic Taylor.

How does it feel to be the top paid running back of the NFL?" she asked as they shared a hug and then smiled at each other.

"Well, I don't know about being the top paid, but it feels good to be back home and playing for the *Chicago Bears*," Dominic replied.

"You didn't like playing for Dallas?" she asked as they walked over to an empty corner in the lounge area.

"Dallas was cool, but I became homesick. Plus, now that I've seen you again, I'm glad to be back home," he replied as he winked, causing her heart rate to quicken and her smile to brighten.

"Is that so? I see you're still a smooth talker," she stated as she leaned back against the wall with him standing in front of her.

"I'm just speaking the truth. I must say your man must be crazy to let you out of his sight looking this good," he replied his glance roaming lazily over her, caused her to shake her head and chuckle at his corny pickup line.

"You still haven't changed, and for your information, I'm single," she said. His smile immediately brightened.

"In that case, will you give me a chance to show you that I have changed and give us a chance to get to know each other again?" he asked as he gently grabbed her hand and kissed the back of it causing her breath to hitch.

"Since you asked so nicely, I don't see why not," she replied as she pulled her business card out of her purse and handed it to him.

"You will not regret it, and here's my card so you can reach me. I'll call you later so we can get together and catch up," he said as he stepped closer to her, and she could smell his woody scented cologne that made her want to step closer to him.

"I'm looking forward to it," she replied before she kissed his cheek, and then winked at him before walking back to her group. She could feel his eyes on her ass causing her to add a little more shake to her hips.

Maybe things are starting to look up for my love life after all, she thought as her smile brightened. When she glanced back, she found Dominic watching her with a smile on his face.

Chapter Six

Walking into his two-level, three-bedroom penthouse after another busy day, Desmond was glad that he got to unwind and watch the Bulls play with his brothers, Ryder, two years his junior and his brother-in-law, Adam, who was thirty-eight. Entering his master bedroom, Desmond started changing from his jeans and polo shirt into a pair of tan cargo shorts and a wife beater. He realized how much he missed hanging out with the guys. Just drinking a cold beer, eating junk food, and watching sports without thinking about work, relationships, or drama.

After he had finished getting dressed, Desmond walked downstairs, and headed to the kitchen. Desmond couldn't stop himself from wondering if Kamala and the ladies were having a fun time at the club. He had been out with them a few times, and he knew after they had a few drinks anything could happen. Then he remembered the ladies had their security teams with them just in case something crazy happened. Walking over to the pantry, Desmond pulled out bags of chips, popcorn, and pretzels and then started to pour them each into large bowls. Then he reached into the refrigerator and pulled out the tray of sandwiches that his housekeeper, Mrs. London had left for them.

Mrs. London had worked for him for years and had become like a second mother to him and his family. He had hired Mrs. London when his busy schedule started interfering with his housekeeping duties, and when she came for her interview, she reminded him so much of Mary Poppins. Still to that day, they still joked about her take-charge attitude and her British accent. Mrs. London and her husband, Eddie were from London and had moved to Chicago to be closer to their family.

Desmond started to carry the food into his man cave that had all the latest video games and systems, a pool table, a dartboard, and two recliner sofas with a large eighty-inch Smart TV hanging on the wall, for the perfect view of the game. Looking around the room, Desmond was proud of his accomplishments because growing up his parents, William, and Aubrey Fleming, both successful accountants had always instilled the values of hard work and a drive for success. They were so proud that he had finished his education with honors and was living his dream of having a career in the music industry.

Walking back to the kitchen for the last of the food, Desmond couldn't help feeling sad that his parents had missed Kingsley getting married. They won't be able to see their first grandchild being born or be in his or her life.

Shaking his head, he couldn't stop himself from thinking of the last time he had seen his parents alive. His family had gone to Gibson's to celebrate Ryder graduating from college. Then he remembered as they were leaving the restaurant, he had hugged both of his parents before they stepped into their car, and he and his siblings had watched as they had driven away.

Then a couple hours later while he was at the studio, Kingsley had called him crying and telling him that he needed to get to the hospital. Rushing to the hospital with Tazmin and Kamala at his side, since they were working together when he got the call, Desmond ran into the E.R. where he was greeted by the scene of his sister crying hysterically while Adam was holding her and crying himself.

Ryder was crying as Lucy Green; his then girlfriend was holding him. When he asked what had happened, his sister told him that their parents had been hit by an eighteen-wheeler truck after the driver had fallen asleep at the wheel. Desmond felt as if his entire world has shifted on its side.

Walking back into his game room with the last of the food, Desmond recalled how Kamala had never left his side as they arranged his parents' funeral or when they filed the lawsuit against the trucking company.

Tazmin and her family had been there also, and Demetria had been a tremendous help with the lawsuit. After Demetria was through with the trucking company, they settled for thirteen million dollars. Between the settlement and the large insurance policies, his parents had left behind, Desmond and his siblings knew they would be alright financially.

After arranging everything on the coffee table, Desmond walked over to the bar. Then he pulled out three Coronas just as his doorbell rang, "Right on time!" he stated as he quickly put the beers on the coffee table and headed it to the front door.

When he opened the front door with a smile on his face, it quickly changed to a frown when he noticed Riley standing there with his family.

He waved everyone in. "Guys everything is in the game room, so go ahead and help yourselves. I'll be right there in a few minutes," Desmond said as he noticed the frown on Ryder and Adam's faces when they looked at Riley.

"That's cool! It's nice to see you again Riley," Ryder replied before he and Adam headed down the hallway shaking their heads and talking to each other.

Desmond already knew they were going to rag on him for Riley being there.

Looking at Riley, he found her smiling up at him, and Desmond was confused as hell, and he wondered why she was there. "Riley, what are you doing here? I told you I had plans tonight," he asked as he crossed his arms over his chest.

"Baby, I was hoping that you wouldn't mind if I joined you and the guys. That way, we can still spend time together," she replied as she walked up to him and put her arms around his waist.

Sighing and dropping his arms, "I'm sorry, but tonight is for me to spend time with my brothers and catch up with them. We can do something tomorrow night," Desmond said as he tried to keep his annoyance out of his voice.

Looking up at him with a pout on her full lips, "It's alright, I understand you need time with the guys. I will see you tomorrow for lunch," she replied before she kissed him.

Seeing that pout on her lips used to turn him on instantly, but in that moment, it just started to annoy the hell out of him, and he had to resist the urge to roll his eyes. As he tried to enjoy the kiss, all he wanted to do was push her away from him, because it felt wrong.

Taking a deep breath as he leaned back, "I'll call you later about lunch tomorrow," he said before he kissed her forehead and then opened the door for her.

"Alright, enjoy your guys' night," she replied as she ran her hand down his chest before walking out the door.

Closing the door, Desmond inhaled deeply, just as he heard laughter echoed throughout the house. When he looked up; Desmond saw Ryder and Adam laughing so hard they had tears running down their faces.

"What's so damn funny?" Desmond asked as he stalked pass them toward the game room. They started following him still laughing.

"Man, you should have seen your face when you opened the door for us and saw Riley standing there. It was as if someone had just told you that you were dying," Ryder joked.

They walked into the game room, and Desmond sat in the middle recliner with Adam on his left and Ryder on his right.

"Then to make it even worse, when she kissed you, your face looked as if you were kissing a frog or something," Adam joked causing Desmond the chuckle.

"With a woman that fine, you looked like you would rather kiss anything but her, so what's going on?" Ryder asked as he turned on the game but muted it during the pre-game interviews.

Shaking his head and sighing, "To be honest, I'm just not feeling Riley on a romantic level anymore. Don't get me wrong, she's a great woman, but I'm not sure she's the woman for me," Desmond replied before picking up his beer and taking a swallow.

"What's changed in the few months that you two have been dating?" Adam asked before he reached for his bottleneck.

Pausing to get his thoughts together and take another sip of his beer, "For one, she's becoming too needy, and all we do is stuff she likes. Then when we are together, all she talks about is her job, and I can't get a word in," Desmond replied shaking his head.   "Man, you two are still in the early stages of dating, give it some time," Ryder suggested before taking another sip of his beer.

"But that's the thing! I don't want to waste our time if I know that she's not the woman I want to be with," Desmond confessed as he looked at his brothers.

"If Riley isn't the woman for you, then who do you have in mind?" Ryder asked smiling.

"I think I already know," Adam said smiling also.

"Who, Mr. know-it-all?" Desmond asked before he took another sip of his beer.

"Kingsley, Ryder, and I have been saying for years that you need to stop window shopping with all those women. You need to settle down with Kamala," Adam replied causing Desmond to choke on the beer he was swallowing.

Patting Desmond on his back, "We all see the way you two look at each other.

"Plus, Kamala is like one of the family," Ryder added before finishing his beer, then headed to the bar and retrieved them each another beer.

"To be honest, I have been thinking about Kamala a lot lately, but I just don't know what to do about it," Desmond replied before finishing his beer also.

"What you need to do is talk to her before another man swoops in and gets her first," Adam suggested before he put his empty beer bottle and theirs in the trash.

"Alright, Bro! While you are playing the guessing game, another man is going to be dating her right under your nose," Ryder stated before grabbing the remote and turning up the volume as the game started.

"I know what I need to do," Desmond replied as he leaned back into his recliner and started to think of what he would say when he next talked to Kamala.

Feeling himself being blindfolded, Desmond started to panic until he felt two soft hands on his chest pushing him back down on his bed. Taking a deep breath as he tried to get his bearings, Desmond felt his other senses come alive as he smelt a familiar scent, but he couldn't place where he knew it from. He could also hear soft jazz playing in the background, which seemed to soothe him some. Turning his head from side to side, he tried to hear where his mystery woman was before he felt her straddle his waist.

When her warm center press down on his manhood, causing Desmond to gasp, and he felt his member twitch in response to such a glorious feeling. He also realized that his pajama bottoms had been removed and that they were skin to skin, causing his breath to hitch. Wanting to touch her, Desmond tried to move his hands, but he realized they were bound to his headboard. Trying not to panic, he took another deep breath just before he felt her hands starting to caress his chest as she slowly grinded her womanhood against his member, which had begun to harden.

The heat radiating from her body and the glorious feeling of her hot and wet folds gliding against his member caused Desmond to groan as his head started to thrash back and forth on his pillow.

The next thing Desmond knew, he felt her warm mouth latch onto his nipples causing him to pull against the restraints as the erotic pleasure she was causing became too much for his brain to handle. Feeling her lick and nibble on his hard and sensitive nipples, sent shockwaves of pleasure straight down to his member that kept twitching against her womanhood earning a moan from his mystery woman. Needing more, Desmond started to increase the pressure as he grinded against her while her kisses moved up to his neck causing him to groan and pull on his restraint.

When she started to increase her movements and the friction of them grinding their pelvises together, Desmond could feel the pressure building up in his nut sack, but he wanted to satisfy her first. Starting to meet her thrusts, he could hear her when she started panting as she nibbled on his ear lobe, he could tell she was close. Hearing how much pleasure she was having, intensified the tension building in his body. When her body became stiff as a board, and she screamed out, Desmond felt the glorious pressure of his release reaching its summit as a loud moan left his lips.

Jumping up in his bed, Desmond looked around the room and realized that the erotic experience was just a dream. Looking down at himself as his heart rate was racing, and he was still gasping for air, he saw that his body was covered with sweat, and his member was rock hard. "What the fuck?" he yelled as he ran his hand through his dreads.

The dream felt so real, and he still could feel her hands caressing his body as he fell back onto the bed and looked at the ceiling. Even though he couldn't make out her face, or figure out who she was, his mystery woman had done things to his body that had his toes curling and his adrenaline pumping through his veins. Her hands were so soft and warm as she caressed his body as if she were trying to memorize every inch of it.

Looking over at his alarm clock and seeing that it was three o'clock in the morning. "Damn I need to get to sleep," he mumbled before he looked down at his rigid member that had tented under his sheets. Desmond knew that the only way to cool down his hot body was a cold shower.

Jumping out of his bed, "This is going to be a long damn day," he mumbled as he headed for his master bathroom.

Chapter Seven

The next week, while sitting in her office, Kamala was trying to focus on the sales reports that she needed to finalize, but she kept thinking about the erotic dreams she kept having. Each night she was waking up drenched in sweat with her womanhood throbbing uncontrollably. Whoever the guy was that was pleasuring her every night, he seemed to know all of her erotic spots and how to make her scream out in pleasure.

Taking a deep breath and tossing the reports down on her desk, Kamala didn't know how she was going to keep going with her womanhood constantly throbbing. Even her nipples were constantly hard and sensitive to the point that when they rubbed against her shirt, she had to hold in her moans.

Then to make matters worse, she had to work with Desmond every day and just seeing his sexy smile caused her body to go into overdrive. She also couldn't forget Dominic, who still had a sex appeal that drew you to him like a starving man at an all you can eat buffet. His deep voice caused her knees to become weak. Crossing her legs to lessen the throbbing, Kamala knew she needed to get laid soon, or she would go out of her mind.

"So I leave town and come back to catch you daydreaming," a female voice yelled causing a smile to come to Kamala's face as she looked up to see Tazmin walking into her office.

"Well if it isn't Mrs. Elliot," Kamala replied smiling as she stood up and hugged her best friend.

"Yes, it is, and what's going on with you?" Tazmin asked as they sat down in the two chairs in front of Kamala's desk.

"Same old thing, work and more work! I want to know about your honeymoon. Did you have a wonderful time?" Kamala asked as she looked at Tazmin. She could see that Tazmin was glowing. Kamala didn't know if it was from her pregnancy or from finally finding true happiness with Adonis.

Chuckling, "To be honest, we were in a honeymoon suite most of the time, but we did take a tour of the Queen Elizabeth II Botanical Park, visited Stingray City and the Sandbar. We had the opportunity to play with friendly southern stingrays. Which you know scared me out of my mind, causing Adonis to laugh at me.

Then I put on my sad face, and he was putty in my hands," Tazmin replied causing the ladies to laugh.

"I'm glad you enjoyed it. Are you ready for the baby's grand entrance?" Kamala asked as she looked down at Tazmin's enlarged belly.

"I wish they would come now! My back and feet are killing me," Tazmin stated causing Kamala to chuckle before she paused when she realized what Tazmin had said.

"Correct me if I'm wrong, but did you say *they*?" Kamala asked as she narrowed her eyes at her best friend.

Smiling, "Yes, you heard correct! I'm having twins and that's what I needed to talk to you about," she replied as she started to rub her belly.

Taking a deep breath, "What's going on? Is something wrong with you or with the babies?" Kamala asked as her heart rate started to race.

Covering Kamala's hand that rested on her lap, "No, we all are fine! Adonis and I just left the doctor's office before we came here. Adonis was headed to the studio while I came to check in with you," Tazmin replied before she leaned back into her chair.

"So if everyone is doing well, what did you need to talk about?" Kamala asked as she narrowed her eyes at Tazmin again when she started smiling.

"Well, Adonis and I were talking about the babies and what would happen to them if something happened to us. So I wanted to ask you if you would be our babies' godmother?" Tazmin asked causing a smile to blossom on Kamala's face before she screamed and hugged Tazmin.

"Of course I'll be their godmother! You have just made my day," Kamala replied as they pulled apart and tears filled her eyes as she also saw Tazmin's eyes filled with tears also.

"Forgive me, I have been crying a lot lately. Thank you for accepting that role in our kids' lives," Tazmin stated as Kamala handed her a tissue from the box on her desk and then proceeded to dry her own eyes.

"Its fine sweetie, we all get emotional at times as you can see from me crying my eyes out now, but I don't care," Kamala joked causing Tazmin to smile.

"Enough about my crazy hormones, tell me about a certain ex-boyfriend popping up," Tazmin suggested as she narrowed her eyes at Kamala causing her to shake her head.

"Leave it to you to get all the juicy details.

Plus, there isn't much to tell. I ran into Dominic Taylor at Club Heat, we talked, and then exchanged numbers. I'm not even sure he will even call," Kamala replied as she leaned back in her chair.

"But if I remember correctly, you told me he was a very charming guy back in the day. So if what I heard was correct about how he was staring at you all that night, then I would bet a year's salary that he will be calling you very soon,"

Tazmin joked. Kamala couldn't do anything but smile and shake her head.

Since she had known Tazmin, she was still amazed at how Tazmin always knew everything while everyone else was left out of the loop.

"Only time will tell! Plus, I have a lot on my plate to stress about instead of worrying about a man. I'm getting eight of our artists ready for the Hot Jamz Tour that we are launching next month," Kamala stated just before her office phone started ringing.

"How about I get my assistant to go grab us some lunch, and then we can sit down and go through it all?" Tazmin suggested as Kamala walked around her desk.

"That would be great if you feel up to it?" Kamala asked as she hit the speaker phone button on her phone.

"I'm fine, I'll see you in a few minutes," Tazmin replied before she walked out the office and shut the door behind her.

"Hello, this is Kamala Hardwood, how can I help you?" she greeted as she sat down in her office chair.

"How about we go to dinner tonight, and we can discuss how we can help each other?" A male voice suggested, and Kamala immediately recognized it as Dominic.

"Still the sweet talker I see," she replied smiling as she heard him chuckle on the other end.

"Like I told you, I'm just telling it like it is, no games or drama. Now back to my question, will you have dinner with me tonight?" he asked causing her to take a deep breath.

"Yes, I will have dinner with you, and it better not be peanut butter and jelly sandwiches like last time," Kamala joked causing Dominic to laugh.

Shaking her head as she remembered their first date when they were in the tenth grade, and they had met at the Naval Pier. For dinner, Dominic had brought a picnic basket with peanut butter and jelly sandwiches and chips.

"Hey, I thought a picnic would impress you, but I promise I will do better tonight," he replied causing her smile to blossom.

"I'm looking forward to it," she stated as she turned her chair to look out at the best view of the Chicago skyline.

"Me too! I'll call you later and don't forget to be ready by seven for a night of fun," Dominic requested.

"I'll be ready! Talk to you later," she replied as she let his deep voice flow over her as she closed her eyes.

"You definitely will!" he added before ending the call.

Opening her eyes, Kamala started to wonder if a night on the town with Dominic was just what the doctor ordered to get her over that funk, she was in. Then she wondered if she should finally talk with Desmond before she started a new chapter in my life with Dominic.

"Only time will tell," she whispered as she turned around to her desk and decided to get some work done.

Chapter Eight

Sitting in the studio working on a few beats for some of his artists, Desmond kept thinking about Kamala. He hadn't seen her all week, but he had heard through the Label grapevine that she had been busy with meetings for the huge tour coming up that would showcase eight of their artists. That was one of the things that he had admired about her, her work ethic. She always wanted to be involved instead of pushing the responsibility on someone else down the corporate ladder.

Shaking his head, Desmond knew he needed to focus and get those beats done, so he could finally go find Kamala and have a much-needed talk. Taking a deep breath with the new determination, he played the new beat he had just finished for Adonis. Then the studio door opened causing him to look up and he saw none other than Adonis himself walk in.

"Damn, I was just finishing up a new beat for you," Desmond greeted as he stood up, and they did a one-armed bro hug.

"My timing is perfect then," Adonis replied as they both sat down in one of the office chairs in front of the soundboard.

"As always! So how does it feel to be a married man?" Desmond asked smiling as he leaned back in his chair.

"I can't even explain it! I'm just blessed that I get to spend the rest of my life with a woman as sexy and smart as Tazmin. Plus waking up with her every morning gives me purpose now," Adonis replied as he leaned back in his chair.

Smiling, "Spoken like a man truly in love," Desmond joked.

"I'll admit that I love Tazmin more than I've ever loved anything in my life. My love for her grows more each day as she grows with my children in her stomach," Adonis stated causing Desmond's eyes to almost popped out of his head as Adonis just chuckled.

"Are you telling me that you two are having more than one baby?" Desmond asked as he stood up and headed over to the bar and grabbed them each a chilled bottle of water before returning to his chair.

Taking the water from Desmond, "We just found out today at her checkup that she's carrying twins," Adonis replied before opening the bottle and taking a sip.

"Congratulations man! You and Tazmin will make great parents," Desmond stated before also taking a sip of his water.

Smiling, "Thanks, man! I almost forgot one of my reasons for stopping by. I need to ask you for a favor," Adonis said as he looked over at Desmond.

Setting his bottle of water down, "You know I have your back, what's up?" Desmond asked.

"Tazmin and I were wondering if you would do us the honor of being our kids' godfather?" Adonis asked causing Desmond to freeze before a smile blossomed on his face.

"Are you serious? Of course I will!" Desmond replied as they bumped fist. "I'm honored that you two even considered me," he continued.

"You are one of our closest friends, and we consider you as a brother," Adonis confessed as he sat his water down on the counter.

"This means a lot to me, and I feel the same about you guys," Desmond stated as he leaned back in his seat.

"Where is Tazmin by the way?" he asked.

"You know Tazmin, she had to check in with everyone. She said she was going to stop by and chat with Kamala and then her sisters," Adonis replied causing Desmond's heart to feel as if it had skipped a beat at the mention of Kamala's name.

"Yes, I do know her like the back of my hand, and I'm not surprised," Desmond added as he chuckled.

"And from the look on your face when I mentioned Kamala's name, you still haven't talked to her yet or are you still seeing Riley?" Adonis asked with a smirk on his face.

Sighing as he ran his hand over his face, "To be honest, I've decided to finally talk to her today just before you walked in. As for Riley, I ended things with her yesterday at lunch," Desmond revealed as he grabbed his water.

"What happened with Riley? I mean when you brought her to the wedding, I thought you two were becoming serious," Adonis mentioned as grabbed his water and took a sip.

"It wasn't just one thing that happened. We weren't meant for each other, and she had become too clingy. She didn't like me spending time with my family and you know that wasn't going to work," Desmond stated as he shook his head.

"I picked up on that the night of the rehearsal dinner before we headed to my bachelor's party. The way she tried to guilt you into staying at the hotel with her and the other ladies," Adonis said as he finished his water and threw the bottle in the trashcan.

"Shit, it got worse after that! She even showed up at my house unannounced, when me and my brothers were having a guy's night. She actually thought I was going to change my plans," Desmond added before he also finished his water.

"Since that's over, what are you going to do about Kamala?" Adonis asked smiling.

"I was going to approach her about it today. So keep your fingers crossed for me," Desmond joked.

"I got you! Now let me hear this new beat you've been working on," Adonis suggested causing Desmond to chuckle at his eagerness.

As he played the track, Desmond hoped that he hadn't waited too late to tell Kamala about his feelings for her.

Later that evening, Desmond was leaving the studio for the day and was headed to Kamala's office. When he walked right into her in the lobby causing his arms to circle around her to keep her from falling backward.

"I was just coming to see you," Desmond greeted causing a beautiful smile to blossom on her full lips as he enjoyed the feel of her body against his.

"Is that so? What was it that you need it? It must have been important to get you out of the studio," she joked causing him to chuckle as he tried to resist the urge to kiss her senseless right before she stepped out of his arms.

"You got jokes today! I was coming to see if you wanted to go out to dinner with me tonight. Especially since we haven't been out in a while," he stated as they walked out of the lobby and arrived at her car where, Kevin and Nicole were waiting. When he looked over at Kamala, he felt as if her gorgeous brown eyes were drawing him in.

"I'm sorry, but I have plans tonight, but we can get together another time," she suggested causing his heart to drop to his toes.

"I understand! Enjoy your night and I'll call you about lunch later," Desmond replied trying to keep the disappointment out of his voice as he saw her smile drop a little when she looked into his eyes.

"Alright, you have a good night and don't do anything I wouldn't do," she joked causing him to shake his head.

"That goes for you too!" he replied as they walked over to her car and Kevin opened the door for her.

"I'll remember that" she stated before kissing his cheek before slipping inside of the car.

Nodding at Kevin and Nicole before they also climbed into the car, he over to his car. Desmond didn't know what his next move was, but he knew that there was no way in hell he was losing Kamala to another man.

Feeling the blindfold covering his eyes, Desmond didn't panic as he had before. Instead, he welcomed the experience with open arms as he then felt his arms being restrained. Inhaling a slow breath, he smelt that amazing scent again as he felt two soft hands caressing up his thighs making their way up his legs causing his hairs on his body to stand up as he moaned.

Trying to resist the urge to move, Desmond inhaled more of the glorious scent that was surrounding him like a cocoon. The moment he exhaled, he felt a warm hand wrap around his member causing him to jump and gasp. All too soon her mesmerizing hand seemed to calm him down as her other hand started to caress his chest. While she started to gently caress his semi-hard member, Desmond had to squeeze his eyes shut as the sensations flowing through his body almost became too much.

With his eyes still closed, he felt the silkiness and warmth of her tongue licking the mushroom head of his member, causing him to gasp as he started pulling against his restraints. The rush of pleasure was almost overpowering, and he didn't know how much more his body could take. Waving his head back and forth, Desmond's body almost jumped off the bed when he felt her hot mouth envelope his member. Releasing a deep groan, Desmond could feel her starting a slow pace as she went up and down while she lavished his member with a powerful suction that had him tongue-tied.

So wrapped up in the sensations flowing through his body, Desmond almost didn't notice when she had removed the blindfold and went back to stroking his member. When he opened his eyes, he recognized that he was still in his bedroom and that she had begun to bob her head up and down on his member again causing him to moan. When he looked down at the beautiful goddess that had given him more pleasure than he could imagine, he was greeted by the beautiful brown eyes that had been haunting him for years.

Jumping up and gasping for air, Desmond ran his hand over his face before looking around his bedroom and realizing he was alone. Taking a deep breath, "It was Kamala all this time," he whispered as he remembered the dream he had just experienced and realized that he was finally able to see the woman's beautiful face. Finally discovering that it was her, made the dream seem more real. Falling back on his pillow and looking down at his hard member, Desmond already knew he had an appointment with another cold shower for the sixth time that week.

"I have got to straighten things out between us before I get a serious case of blue balls," he joked as he threw back his covers and headed for another cold shower.

Chapter Nine

Entering her six-bedroom house and tossing her keys in the bowl on the table in the foyer, Kamala kept replaying the conversation she had with Desmond earlier. Walking in her bedroom to change for her date with Dominic, she couldn't understand why Desmond's whole demeanor changed when he found out she had plans for the evening.

He was dating Riley, and they were just friends, so why did it matter to him so much. Walking into her walk-in closet, she pulled out her indigo flower dress that had a wrap effect bodice, elastic waist to show off her slim waist and a side slit to show her toned legs. Kamala then wondered why Desmond had waited until the day she was going out with Dominic to finally ask her out.

In all the years she had a crush on him, and it seemed as if nobody could compare to Desmond, so all the dates she had been on had never progressed. While Desmond continued to date and live his playboy life. As she started to get dressed, she realized that even though she loved Desmond, she couldn't sacrifice her life and happiness hoping he would return those same feelings. Stepping into her indigo ankle strap heels, Kamala knew that giving Dominic a real chance to get to know her again was the first step in getting over her infatuation with Desmond.

Walking over to her dresser, Kamala opened her jewelry box and pulled out her gold necklace with a Solitaire three karat diamond and the matching earrings. Looking at the set, caused her to remember when Desmond had given it to her for her thirtieth birthday.

Tazmin and Desmond had given her a surprise birthday party at Club Unbelievable, and as a smile came to her face, she remembered all the fun they had as they danced all night long. She could never forget when Desmond pulled her into a private room and gave her the necklace and earrings. Then as she went to hug him, they had ended up kissing. That kiss, even though it was brief, was the best gift she could have gotten on her birthday.

Kamala realized Dominic would be arriving soon. Looking at the set one more time, she dropped it back into the jewelry box. That night was about new beginnings, and she didn't need any reminders of Desmond with her as she tried to move on.

Looking at herself in the full-length mirror, Kamala knew that with her looking that good, Dominic didn't stand a chance. Smiling she whispered, "Tonight, I'm just focusing on having a good time," just as her doorbell rang.

Picking up her indigo purse, and heading downstairs, Kamala became excited to get to spend time with an old friend from her childhood. When she arrived at the door, she took a calming breath, and then opened the door to be greeted by the handsome Dominic Taylor dressed in a black tailor-made suit with a navy silk tie. With his fresh haircut and shave and dazzling smile, Kamala felt her heart rate pick up as she had to resist the urge to lick her lips at the delicious sight.

"Hello Dominic, you are looking handsome as ever," she greeted her smile causing him to smile.

"Hello to you too, and I must say, you look beautiful as always," Dominic replied as Kamala stepped out of the door and locked it behind her.

"Thank you for the compliment! So, what are our plans for tonight?" she asked as they walked down the front walkway.

When she looked at his car and realized it was an Aston Martin Rapide S, her mouth felt as if it had hit the floor.

Chuckling, "I see you like my new car?" he asked while he hit the unlock button on his key ring and opened the door for her.

"You know I have always had a thing for cars, and this car is in a league of its own," she replied as she slid onto the black diamond quilted leather seat.

"That makes two of us," he stated before he closed her door.

Waiting for Dominic to get into the car, Kamala looked around the luxury car and could tell all the interior was handcrafted.

When Dominic slid into the car and shut his door, Kamala's attention was drawn from the luxury car to the sexy driver and his hypnotic cologne. She recognized it was Clive Christian Number One by the distinctive ancient Indian sandalwood and the Arabian Jasmine Sambace scent.

"Do I stink or something?" Dominic asked bringing Kamala out of her thoughts.

Shocked, "What? No, you smell amazing! I just realized what the scent was," she replied as he smiled and started the car with it purring to life.

"Thank you! I found this cologne while I was in London for a vacation, and I've been wearing it ever since," he replied as he looked over at her as he continued to drive.

"Well, it suits you perfectly! And back to my earlier question, where are we going tonight?" Kamala asked as she ran her hand over the soft leather armrest on her door, loving the feel of it against her skin.

"Since I know you don't like surprises and since I want to stay in your good graces, I'll tell you. Tonight, we are having dinner at Fred's at Barneys," he replied bringing a smile to her face as he continued to focus on the road.

"Another excellent choice, you are on a roll tonight. I'm definitely going to have to watch myself around you," she joked causing Dominic to chuckle.

"Kamala, you should know that when you're with me, you will always be taken care of," Dominic stated, and Kamala felt warmth spread within from his declaration.

As they continued to the restaurant, Kamala remembered how close they were in high school. Dominic always made her feel special and was always there for her, even with his busy schedule during football season and the other sports he played. Dominic used to leave love notes in her locker, and he even had the football team serenaded her during their senior year homecoming game.

So wrapped up in her thoughts, Kamala hadn't realized they had arrived at the restaurant until the valet had opened her door, as Dominic came around the car and then offered her his hand. Kamala had to remind herself to take calming breaths and just go with the evening.

The moment she placed her hand into Dominic's warm and strong hand, Kamala had to resist the urge to moan because his touch sent a shiver down her spine. Still holding her hand, Dominic led her into the restaurant, and after giving the hostesses his name, they were quickly shown to a table where they had a perfect view of Lake Michigan.

After taking in the beautiful view and she looked around the dining room at the starched white tablecloths and its contemporary and rich decor. Kamala knew that it was going to be a restaurant that she and the girls would be coming to very often.

"Dominic, thank you for bringing me here. I have wanted to come here for a long time, but with my schedule it's kind of hard," Kamala stated as she looked across the candlelit table into Dominic's beautiful gray eyes.

"It's my pleasure. Plus I had to step up my game from the peanut butter and jelly sandwiches," Dominic joked and then chuckled.

"You know what? Now that I look back on our dates back then, they were so sweet and romantic for a couple of teenagers," she added as she felt herself being drawn in by his gorgeous eyes and smile.

"Welcome to Fred's at Barneys and I'm Jason, and I'll be your waiter this evening. Let me start by getting your drink and appetizer order," Jason greeted before his eyes almost popped out of his head when he looked down at them and realized who they were.

"Thank you, Jason, and I'll just have an Appletini," Kamala replied smiling.

"And I'll have a sweet tea," Dominic added as he took the menu Jason had offered him.

"Alright, I'll go get your drinks and be right back," Jason stated before he walked away.

Chuckling, "It's still funny to me how people act around me, but I guess you are used to it Mr. Superstar," Kamala joked as she looked at her menu.

"It used to freak me out at first, but now I'm used to it, and I love meeting my fans. I'm not surprised that you draw people's attention," Dominic stated as a warm smile lit up his face.

"Is that so? Why is that?" she asked as she sat her menu down on the table giving him her full attention.

"To be honest, Kamala when I met you in tenth grade, I had a huge crush on you. Then when I finally got up the nerve to ask you out and you accepted, I could have jumped over the moon. Then last week, after not seeing you for so many years and when I finally did, all those old feelings resurfaced. Plus, you are still the most beautiful woman to me," he confessed causing her to blush again when she noticed his eyes getting darker as he looked across the table at her.

"Here are your drinks and if you're ready I'll take your entree order," Jason requested after he walked up to the table. Then he put their drinks in front of them and putting their conversation on hold.

"Ladies first," Dominic replied as he smiled at her.

"I'll have the New York striploin," Kamala stated as she handed Jason her menu.

"And I'll have the chicken parmesan," Dominic added as he also handed Jason his menu.

"Alright, enjoy your drinks and I'll be back shortly with your dinner," Jason replied before walking away.

"Back to our conversation, Kamala I didn't mean to make you feel uncomfortable by what I just said," Dominic stated looking across the table at her.

Sighing, "Dominic, you didn't make me uncomfortable, and just so you know that I also had a crush on you too back in high school before we started dating. I also feel I owe you an apology for the way things ended between us," Kamala stated as she felt a little uneasy bringing up the sensitive subject that had haunted her for so many years.

After taking a sip of his tea, he said, "I always wondered why you ended our relationship so fast after we went to college," Dominic said giving her his full attention.

"When you left for college in Miami and I remained here in Chicago, I realized that long distance relationships don't work out. Plus, I felt I was holding you back from your dream of having a great football career," she revealed before taking a sip of her drink since her mouth suddenly felt dry as the desert.

"Kamala, all you had to do was talk to me and we could have worked it out. You were the best thing in my life, and I could have gone to any school, even here in Chicago,"

Dominic revealed as he covered her hand that was lying on the table.

His touch seemed to calm her mind from its racing thoughts, but it caused her body to hum with desire.

"Maybe I should have talked to you, but I just didn't want you to resent me for holding you back," Kamala replied.

Looking over at her and caressing her hand, "How about we start fresh tonight and get to know each other again. We also need to promise to be honest with each other and talk about any issues that may come," Dominic suggested bringing a smile to her lips as she released a sigh of relief.

"I can agree to that! Now, tell me how it feels to be playing for the Bears?" she asked causing him to smile also.

As they enjoyed great food and great conversation while getting to know each other again, Kamala was glad she had gone to Club Heat and ran into Dominic after all.

Chapter Ten

Sitting in the boardroom the following Monday, waiting for Tazmin and the Vice-Presidents to arrive, Kamala thought about Dominic and their great date. During dinner, it felt like old times as they talked and laughed about their times together in high school and their experiences in college. Just spending a couple hours with Dominic, seemed to make her forget about the stress in her life and for once she had a fun time.

"That must have been a great daydream, from the big smile on your face," a female voice said pulling Kamala from her thoughts to realize Tazmin had arrived along with her sisters.

"For your information, I was just thinking about the wonderful time I had with Dominic, Friday night," Kamala replied just as the rest of the group walked into the room.

"You know that you have to tell us about this date over lunch?" Demetria asked as everyone began to take their seats.

"That's fine with me! I don't have any meetings for the rest of the day," Kamala replied just as she looked up to see Desmond walk into the room with his eyes focused on her.

"Alright, now that everyone has arrived, let's get this meeting started," Tazmin greeted as she sat down in her seat at the head of the table.

"Before we start, I want to thank everyone for all your hard work while I was gone. I also heard we have a few new artists joining the family," Tazmin continued as she looked around the table.

Smiling along with everyone else at the table, Kamala found it hard to focus on the meeting since Desmond kept staring at her.

"Tazmin is correct! Which is why Desmond was invited to the meeting because I want you each to listen to their sound. Then figure out how your department will help them further their career," Reyna added as she looked around the table.

"We are going to start with a rapper called Malik. I'm sure most of you already know of him," Rozlynn stated before she hit the play button on the remote to the sound system.

As they listened to the masterful skills flowing from that young man's mouth, Kamala remembered how successful his show had been at Club Heat. After meeting him and getting to know him, despite his hardcore lyrics, he came off as a true gentleman and complete opposite of the rapper stereotype. As the last song finished playing, Kamala looked around the table to see everyone already writing down ideas.

"So what does everyone think?" Kamala asked.

"After seeing him perform at Club Heat and now hearing some more of his music, I think he could go far in the industry," Livia replied as she leaned back in her chair.

"I agree! He has great potential and with some fine tuning from Desmond, his music could take him to the next level," Malia added causing everyone to look at Desmond as he continued to write down ideas.

"So Desmond, what do you think of Malik?" Tazmin asked.

Clearing his throat and looking over at Tazmin, he said, "To be honest, since he started rapping, I've been following his career, and I'm honored to work with him. I also agree with Malia, that with some fine tuning and great beats he could reach the next level." Desmond then looked around the table with his eyes pausing on Kamala.

"Alright, let's hear Grayson Banner's music and then we will listen to Jericho Lender's music. I'm sure you all know these two artists. They decided to change Labels and we welcomed them into our family," Tazmin stated as Kamala watched her constantly rubbing her stomach, which made her a little bit worried about her condition.

As they listened to a few songs from both artists, Kamala remembered all the meetings her and Demetria had with both artists to get their contracts finalized and how relieved they were to be with a new Label.

Taking a few notes of ideas she had for each artists, Kamala looked up as the last song ended to see Desmond smiling at her and then he winked at her causing her to shake her head.

"So how does everyone feel about our new R&B Superstars?" Tazmin asked as she looked around the room.

"Since they both have a huge fan base already, we need to focus on trying new avenues to get new followers, and with a new sound it may also help," Cheyenne stated.

"I agree! They both have unique voices. So why not focus on that instead of trying to make them sound like everyone else in the industry like their old Label had tried and failed miserably," Kamala said as she leaned back in her chair.

"Desmond, do you have any input on the music end?" Tazmin asked.

"I agree with Kamala! They just need the right music and coaching to bring out their uniqueness and the talent they have," he replied.

"So, I need everyone to send a detailed report about your department's plans for each artist to me and Kamala by the end of the week. The last thing that needs to be discussed is the Hot Jamz Tour. How is that coming along?" Tazmin asked.

"On my end, everything is finalized as for the budget, locations, promotion, and the artists have been selected and reserved," Kamala replied. Then she looked in her folder and started to pass everyone a copy of her report.

"As for the promotion, that's already in full swing and ticket sales are already doing great," Livia added.

"It seems as if everything is in order, so just keep up the excellent work and we will meet again next week," Tazmin said dismissing the group.

Kamala started to collect her papers and put them in her briefcase when she noticed that Desmond had moved to the chair to her left.

"How have you been Ms. Hardwood?" Desmond asked causing a smile to develop on her face.

"I'm doing great Mr. Flemings, how was your weekend?" she asked as she laid her full briefcase on the table and turned her chair toward him to give him her full attention.

"I didn't do much! Just spend time with my family and then spent the rest of the time getting some much-needed rest," Desmond replied causing her to imagine him in his bed naked looking sexy as hell.

"I understand, I did the same thing all weekend after I did some shopping," she stated as she felt herself getting lost in his eyes.

"So how was your date Friday?" he asked causing her heart to race.

Clearing her throat, "It was great! He was someone I had dated in high school and we just caught up and got to know each other again," Kamala said as she noticed that his nostrils had started to flare ever so slightly.

"I'm glad you had a great time, and I'll get up with you later about our lunch date. I need to get going, I'm late for my recording session with Adonis in the studio," he stated before he stood up and she stood also.

"I understand, and I may stop by after me and the ladies get back from lunch," she added as she noticed her group waiting for her.

"I'm looking forward to it," he replied before he walked out of the room causing her to release a shaky breath.

Looking around the room, Kamala noticed her friends looking at her with a smirk on their faces. Rolling her eyes and picking up her briefcase, Kamala knew they were going to ask a million questions at lunch.

"Kamala, you are my idol!" Reyna joked causing the group to laugh after Kamala told them about her date with Dominic.

"What are you talking about?" Kamala asked before taking a sip of her *Long Island Iced Tea*, which was why she loved coming to Morton's Steakhouse.

"Here you are with not one but two sexy and successful men beating down your door," Reyna replied causing Kamala to shake her head.

"What in the hell are you talking about?" Kamala asked causing the group to start laughing at the confused look on her face.

"Come on Kamala, you have Dominic Taylor, Mr. MVP taking you out to dinner. Then you have Desmond following you around like a lost puppy," Demetria joked before taking a sip of her margarita.

"She has a point! Dominic entering into the picture seemed to jumpstart Desmond into action," Rozlynn said smiling.

Shaking her head, "You guys have it all wrong! Yes, I really enjoyed spending time with Dominic and being with him brought up a lot of old feelings. As far as Desmond is concerned, he's dating Riley and doesn't have any romantic feelings toward me," Kamala stated before gulping down the rest of her drink.

"Kamala, when I say this, I mean it as nicely as possible, but are you blind or do you have your head in the sand?" Reyna asked causing Kamala to roll her eyes as she signaled their waiter for another round of drinks.

"Kamala, since I'm close to both of you, I've tried to stay neutral. You have to know that Desmond ended things with Riley last week," Tazmin revealed just as she frowned and rubbed her stomach again.

"Tazmin, are you feeling alright?" Reyna asked as they all looked at Tazmin with frowns on their faces.

Continuing to rub her stomach, "Yeah, I'm fine, I'm just having Braxton Hicks' contractions. The doctor told us that it was normal. Now back to Ms. Hardwood and her love triangle," Tazmin joked smiling.

"Very funny! Guys, Desmond doesn't have feelings for me, and if he did, he has had many years to tell me. Now that I'm seeing Dominic, that's where I'm going to put my focus," Kamala stated just as Tazmin gasped and then jumped up.

"Tazmin, are you alright? Do we need to call Adonis or your doctor?" Kamala asked racing around the table as she put her arm around Tazmin as she gasped again.

"Guys, my water just broke!" Tazmin yelled as another contraction hit her.

"Demetria, call Adonis and her doctor! Reyna hurry to get your car! We need to head to the hospital," Kamala said as she started to lead Tazmin out of the restaurant with her sisters following behind them.

As they quickly got Tazmin into the car, Kamala prayed that her friend and godchildren made it through the delivery safely.

Chapter Eleven

Pulling up to Northwestern Memorial Hospital, Kamala held Tazmin's hand as she continued to breathe through her contractions as they started to come every five to ten minutes. Looking out the window, she saw Adonis, Desmond, and a nurse standing at the entrance causing her to sigh out of relief.

"We are at the hospital, and Adonis is here," Kamala revealed as she wiped Tazmin's forehead with a napkin.

"Thank you so much for helping me!" Tazmin gasped as another contraction hit her causing her to squeeze Kamala's hand.

Then the back door opened and Rozlynn jumped out of the car to be replaced by Adonis.

"What are sisters for?" Kamala replied as she kissed Tazmin's forehead.

"Baby I'm here! I'm going to lift you out of the car over to the wheelchair," Adonis stated before he kissed Tazmin on her lips.

"Baby, that's fine!" Tazmin replied sounding so tired and Kamala started to worry.

"Adonis, you need to move her now before her next contraction hits," Kamala suggested as she wiped Tazmin's forehead again.

"Thank you! Alright, baby let's go!" he suggested as he picked Tazmin up as if she weighed ten pounds and softly sat her down in the wheelchair. Then the nurse rushed through the hospital lobby with everyone following her until she came to a set of doors saying restricted area.

"You guys are welcome to wait in the waiting room, as we get mom and dad settled in the delivery room," the short Caucasian nurse stated before pushing Tazmin through the door.

Taking a deep breath and running her hands through her soft curls, Kamala led the group to the waiting room, where they all sat down in a cluster of chairs.

"This is so nerve wrecking!" Reyna yelled as she leaned back in the chair.

"I've never seen Tazmin in so much pain before," Alondra added as she wiped the corner of her eye, causing Kamala to hug her.

"Guys, you know that Tazmin is one of the strongest people we know. She and those babies will be fine," Kamala declared as she passed tissues to all of Tazmin's sisters when she realized they all had tears in their eyes.

"Does anyone want any coffee? I need something to calm my nerves," Demetria joked causing the group to chuckle.

"Yeah, I'll go with you!" Reyna added.

"Me too! Kamala and Desmond, do you want some coffee?" Alondra asked causing Kamala to remember that Desmond was even there.

Shaking her head, "No I'm fine," Kamala replied before she walked over to the window that had a view of the front of the hospital.

"I'm fine too," Desmond replied.

Looking out the window, "Lord, I pray that you watch over my friend and those babies," Kamala prayed as she fought back the tears flooding her eyes.
Taking a deep breath as she became lost in her thoughts as time passed by, she soon felt someone standing behind her and when she looked over her left shoulder, she saw that it was Desmond.

"Are you alright?" he asked as he stood beside her, and she turned to face him.

Taking a deep breath, "Yes, I'm fine! I'm just a little worried about Tazmin and the babies," she replied as she looked back out the window, looking at nothing in particular.

"Tazmin is as strong and stubborn as a mule, so she will get through this and be back to work by 5 o'clock," Desmond joked causing Kamala to chuckle.

"You do have a point there, and I wouldn't be surprised if she decided to have a meeting in the delivery room," Kamala added causing them both to laugh.

"Plus, if my godchildren are anything like their parents, they will be just as stubborn and focused," Desmond stated causing Kamala to pause.

"They asked you to be their godparent too?" Kamala asked with a frown on her face.

"Yes, Adonis asked me. Why?" he asked as he leaned against the wall.

"Tazmin asked me too," she replied.

"Do you realize that we'll be meeting our godchildren in the next few hours?" Desmond asked smiling.

"Yes, we will, and I can't wait to spoil them," Kamala said smiling as she made a mental note of all the stuff she needed to get for the babies.

"I can see those wheels turning in that beautiful head of yours, and I feel sorry for those baby stores when you and the Foster sisters are done shopping," Desmond joked causing her to chuckle.

"We heard that Desmond," Alondra said as she lightly hit him on his arm.

"We all know it's the truth," Desmond replied as they returned to their chairs just as Adonis's brothers and cousin walked into the room.

"Hey guys, how is Tazmin?" Spencer asked as he hugged all the ladies and bumped fist with Desmond.

"They took her into the delivery room about an hour ago. So now we just have to play the waiting game," Demetria replied as Spencer sat down beside her.

"How long does delivery normally last?" Rico asked as he hugged Kamala next.

"It varies, it can last an hour to forty-eight hours," Kamala replied causing the guys to whistle and shake their heads.

"I don't see how you women can do it! Being in pain for so long for something the size of a watermelon to fit through a hole the size of a lemon," Gunner stated causing the guys to shutter in their seats.

"It is painful, but all the work is worth it when you hold your baby in your arms," Alondra stated causing the ladies to smile.

"Don't any of you want kids of your own someday?" Demetria asked looking at the guys.

"I never really thought about it, but with the right woman anything is possible," Liam replied.

"I always wanted a big family with the woman I would marry," Desmond added.

Kamala looked away as she realized with things the way they were between them at that moment, that woman wouldn't be her.

"What about you Kamala? How many kids do you want?" Demetria asked with a smirk on her face when Kamala look at her.

"I always wanted a big family too! Being the only child, I realize how important it is to have siblings," she replied as she looked around the group until she came to Desmond who was looking at her smiling.

"Adonis!" Demetria yelled causing everyone to turn around to see him walking toward them dressed in blue scrubs with a huge smile on his face.

"How's Tazmin and the babies?" Spencer asked as everyone hugged Adonis.

"Tazmin and our identical sons are doing great!" Adonis revealed causing tears to come to Kamala's eyes as she hugged him last.

Chapter Twelve

Excitement coursing through her veins, Kamala pushed the hospital door open to be greeted by the beautiful sight of Tazmin holding two bundles wrapped in blue blankets.

"Hello, Mommy!" Kamala joked causing a smile to blossom on Tazmin's face when she looked up at her.

"Hello, Godmother!" Tazmin replied as Kamala walked closer to the bed and looked down at the most beautiful babies she had ever seen.

"They are so cute!" Kamala whispered when she realized both of the babies were sleeping with their cute button noses.

"Thank you! Do you want to hold one of them?" Tazmin asked causing Kamala to get a little nervous at the thought of holding something so small and delicate.

"Sure!" Kamala replied as Tazmin lifted up the baby in her right arm. Then Kamala very carefully lifted him up to her chest causing the baby to stir from his sleep, but he quickly settled down once she nestled him in her arm.

"He's so small!" Kamala whispered as she ran her finger over his soft cheek.

"He sure as hell didn't feel small coming out," Tazmin joked causing Kamala to chuckle as she sat down in the chair that was sitting beside the bed.

"I can't imagine the pain. Was the delivery that bad?" Kamala asked.

"To be honest, after hearing all the childbirth horror stories, my labor was a breeze. Some women are in labor for hours, whereas mine only lasted an hour," Tazmin stated as she looked down at the baby in her arms.

"I'm just glad that you all are healthy and made it through," Kamala said as she smiled at her friend.

"Me too! Halfway through I felt so tired but, Adonis kept me focused and motivated me through it," Tazmin replied smiling.

"You are truly blessed to have a loving husband and two beautiful sons," Kamala said causing Tazmin to nod her head in agreement.

"I agree! This is just the beginning for us," Tazmin replied as she looked at her babies.   "How many more kids do you two want?" Kamala asked as the baby wrapped his little hand around her finger as she caressed his little hand.

"We talked about having four kids and we're ahead of the game now. So I only have to go through this two more times, but it'll be worth it," Tazmin replied as she looked down at her son in her arms smiling.

"Have you decided on names yet?" Kamala asked.

"Yes, we have, but I wanted to tell you and Desmond together since you both are their godparents," Tazmin replied just as the door opened, and Adonis and Desmond walked into the room.

"Right on time as usual," Tazmin joked while Adonis walked over and kissed her, and then he looked down at his son smiling.

"On time for what?" Adonis asked as he sat down on the bed with Tazmin and put his arm around her, causing a bright smile to blossom on her face.

Seeing them together warmed Kamala's heart, after remembering all the hurdles they had to jump over to get to that moment.

"I was telling Kamala that we wanted to tell her and Desmond together what the babies' names were," Tazmin replied as Desmond hugged her. Then he pulled up a chair next to Kamala and sat down.

"Alright, the suspense is killing me! What are their names?" Kamala asked causing everyone in the room the chuckle.

"The baby you're holding is Hayden Isaiah Elliott, and this little guy is Hunter Isaac Elliott," Tazmin replied as tears came to

Kamala's eyes as she looked down at Hayden.

"Desmond, would you like to hold your godson?" Tazmin asked causing a scared look to cross his face, which had everyone laughing as Kamala wiped away her tears. "Sure!" he replied as he stood up, and Tazmin placed Hunter in his arms.

While Desmond sat back down in his chair, Hunter woke up and looked up at him with the most vibrate gray eyes Kamala had ever seen.

"He is so light," Desmond whispered as he played with the baby's hand, causing Hunter to smile.

"Hayden weighed seven and a half pounds and Hunter weighed seven pounds, so that's about average weight for a newborn baby," Tazmin replied as Kamala felt her eyes almost pop out of her head.

"You are my hero! To go through all that and still have energy left over," Kamala joked as Hayden started to wake up, and she started to rock him back and forth gently.

"Don't even start on the labor! Tazmin was a champ through it all, but when I saw the head come out, I will admit I got a little lightheaded," Adonis joked causing the group to laugh.

"I feel you on that! How was it with the cutting the cord part?" Desmond asked as he continued playing with Hunter.

"With everything happening so quickly, I didn't have a chance to think about it," Adonis replied as he tightened his arm around Tazmin.

"For him it was quick, but for me it felt like hours. Which is why I'm so glad he was here," Tazmin replied as she looked up at her husband, earning her a kiss.

Seeing their affection for each other gave Kamala hope for finding a man to give her his love and affection. When she looked over at Desmond, she found him looking at her with an unknown emotion floating around his eyes, but it quickly changed when he smiled at her. Kamala almost thought she had imagined the look in his eyes. As she watched him look down at Hunter, she began to wonder if Desmond really wanted a family of his own or did he enjoy living the rich and famous bachelor life.

Hearing Tazmin yawn, "It looks like someone is tired, and that's our queue to let mommy get some rest," Kamala stated as she stood up.

"I am getting sleepy, but you don't have to leave," Tazmin replied as Kamala handed Hayden to her and then hugged her.

"Yes, we do so that you can get some rest," Desmond stated as he handed Hunter to Adonis.

"We'll be back tomorrow, but right now I need to go shopping for my god babies," Kamala joked causing Tazmin to chuckle while the guys shook their heads.

"There will be nothing left on the shelves," Desmond joked causing Kamala to elbow him in his side.

"Don't leave out Adonis's family and you at the toy stores," Tazmin joked causing a blush to rise in Desmond's cheeks.

"To be honest, I was going to buy a few things today," Desmond stated causing Kamala to shake her head.

Hugging Tazmin and Adonis, "We'll see you guys tomorrow. Adonis, make sure she gets some rest and to try not to focus on work," Kamala suggested as she walked over to the door.

"I will. Plus, I have all her electronic devices, so she can't work," Adonis replied earning him an elbow in his side from Tazmin, causing Kamala to chuckle.

Then Desmond hugged Tazmin and bumped his fist with Adonis's before following Kamala to the door.

"I like how you two are talking about me like I'm not here," Tazmin grumbled causing the group to laugh more.

"You just focused on resting, I have the Label covered," Kamala replied.

"I know, and I love you, Sis," Tazmin stated.

"I love you too," Kamala replied before she walked out of the room followed by Desmond.

Walking down the hallway, "How does it feel to be a godfather?" Kamala asked as she looked at him to see a smile slowly developing on his lips.

"It's still surreal to me, and holding Hunter made me realize what's important in life," Desmond replied looking at her with that strange look in his eyes again.

Taking a deep breath, "I understand what you mean because just holding little Hayden made me want to be a mother myself someday," Kamala stated just as they arrived at the front of the hospital.

"Damn, I need to call Kevin! I forgot that I rode here with Reyna," Kamala continued as she pulled out her cell phone.

"You don't have to call Kevin; I'll give you a lift home," Desmond suggested causing her to look up at him with a frown on her face.

Sighing, "Thank you for offering, but I don't want to inconvenience you," she stated just before Desmond gently grabbed her hand.

"It's fine, plus I wouldn't have offered if I didn't want to do it," he said as he led her to the parking lot.

With him holding her hand, Kamala wasn't prepared for the erotic thoughts running through her mind. So she prayed that she made it home without doing or saying something crazy.

Riding in the passenger seat of Desmond's Escalade, Kamala felt like she was sitting on pins and needles.

"Kamala, breathe before you pass out," Desmond joked causing her to sigh as she leaned back into the seat.

"I'm breathing, what are you talking about?" she asked as she looked over at him.

"You're sitting over there as if I was going to bite you," Desmond said as he looked over at her.

"I see you got jokes, and for your information I was just thinking about Tazmin and Adonis," Kamala replied as she looked out of the car window.

"What about them?" Desmond asked as he focused on the road.

"After all the hell they went through in their past, they were able to find true love and was willing to fight for it. Now they are happily married with two of the cutest babies in the world," she stated as she pictured the babies in her mind.

"Kamala, you are beautiful and successful woman, who could have any man you wanted. So you will have no problem finding Mr. Right," Desmond stated causing her to look over at him with a frown on her face.

"If you only knew how many frogs I've kissed, only to end up alone and disappointed," she replied before taking a deep breath and looking back out of her window.

"I know what you mean, I've dated a lot of women, but they only saw my job and money," he added as he shook his head.

"Come on, you love the playboy life of partying and gorgeous women falling all over you," Kamala joked as she chuckled.

Sighing, "At first it was fun, but now I want someone I can share everything with and who I can love. I want the type of loving relationship that my sister and Adam have," he replied causing her to look over at him, and she looked into his hypnotic eyes.

Clearing her throat, "Speaking of your sister, how are Kingsley, Adam, and Ryder doing?" she asked as she looked out her window again.

"Kingsley and Adam are doing great and are expecting their first child soon," Desmond replied. When Kamala looked over at him, she could see his eyes light up at the news with a smile coming to his lips.

"That's great! I have to call her tonight and congratulate them. How does it feel to know that you are about to be an uncle?" Kamala asked.

"It feels great! I'm just glad that they are finally becoming parents after so many years of trying," he replied as they turned onto her street.

"Yeah, I know about all the doctors and tests they had to go through," Kamala added.

"I didn't know you and my sister were that close," he stated looking at her.

"Of course we are, and she joins us for ladies night sometimes or when we go shopping," Kamala said smiling as he groaned when she mentioned shopping.

"I should have known shopping was involved," he joked causing her to punch him lightly on his arm.

"Very funny, but shopping helps us relax," she replied.

Pulling up to her house, "I understand, watching a basketball game or playing pool in my game room helps me relax," he said as she unbuckled her seatbelt.

"I didn't know you had a game room at your condo," Kamala stated as she pulled her keys out of her purse.

"That's right you haven't been to my new penthouse since I moved in a few months ago?" Desmond asked.

"No, I haven't, with Tazmin's wedding and everything going on, it's hard to find time to do anything," she replied as she felt like prolonging their conversation.

"How about you come over Friday night for dinner, and I can beat you at a game of pool since you beat me the last time we played?" Desmond asked as he turned in his seat to face her.

Looking into his eyes, Kamala was battling with her mind and body, with each telling her to do something different.

"Sure, why not. Plus, I want to see how you handle this butt whipping," she joked causing him to smile.

"Alright, it's a date then."

"Ok, you drive home safely," she said as she kissed his smooth cheek before she opened the door to get out.

"I will!" he replied just before she climbed out and shut her door.

Walking up the front walkway, Kamala looked over her shoulder to see Desmond watching her. Waving at him, and then turning around, Kamala released a shaky breath. Then she realized she was going on a date with Desmond finally while she was still dating Dominic, *What the hell was I thinking?* she thought as she opened the front door.

Chapter Thirteen

Moaning as she felt him kissing and licking her neck, Kamala realized the amazing heat that she was feeling was from her mystery man as he hovered over her body as she laid on her stomach. Smiling as she enjoyed the way he manipulated her body like a master, Kamala never wanted the moment to end. Feeling his kisses travel down her back, Kamala felt a shiver travel down her spine as she arched her back.

Every second that he spent ravishing her body, Kamala knew she would never forget that experience. As he massaged her muscles and lavished them with kisses, Kamala felt like putty in his hands. Those strong hands slowly moved to her butt, causing her to push up her rear-end into his hands needing more pleasure that only he could provide. Squeezing her eyes closed, her breath hitched when his masterful fingers slide between her legs until he reached the folds of her womanhood.

Gasping, Kamala gripped the sheets so hard that she ripped them off the mattress. The sensations of him manipulating her clit had her so lightheaded, Kamala couldn't tell what was real anymore. Then to increase her pleasure, he applied more pressure to her clit as his other fingers slowly started to enter her opening where she could hear just how wet she was.

Starting to push back against his hand, meeting each of his thrusts forward, Kamala could feel the tension building in her core. Between the sound of her wetness, and the sound of his hand pounding in and out of her body, Kamala became delirious with desire. She felt like she was jumping off a cliff as stars flashed before her eyes and she gasped for air.

With her heart pounding out of her chest, Kamala felt her mystery man gently helping her turn over onto her back, and when she opened her eyes, she saw the last person she expected to see.

"Desmond!" she screamed as she jumped up in her bed breathing heavily. Looking around her room, she realized she just had another erotic dream. As she reached on her nightstand for the glass of water she had left there, she realized that dream was totally different from the rest. That dream didn't seem so rushed, and their lovemaking was so slow and passionate. It seemed as if he was trying to draw out her pleasure to the fullest extent.

Taking a deep breath and setting the glass back on the nightstand with her hand shaking ever so slightly. Kamala ran her hands through her tangled hair as she couldn't get over that her mystery guy turned out to be none other than Desmond of all people. "Is this some kind of joke?" she yelled as she fell back onto her pillows.

Turning on her side and looking over at her alarm clock, Kamala realized that she only had an hour left before she had to get up for work.

"This is going to be a long ass day," she grumbled as she hit her pillow and tried to get comfortable.

Later at her office, Kamala tried to get some of her reports done, but she kept thinking about Desmond and their upcoming date. Then she thought about Dominic and how sweet he was to send her flowers and candy every day. Kamala didn't know how she had gotten herself into that situation. Plus, she realized that maybe her dinner with Desmond was just two friends getting together to hang out. If that was the case, then she was stressing herself out for nothing.

Looking down at the papers scattered on her desk, "I need to focus and get this done," she whispered just as someone knocked on her door.

"Come in!" she yelled as she put her pen down on her desk as the door opened, and Dominic walked in carrying a bouquet of red and white roses.

"Well isn't this a surprise?" she asked as she stood up smiling.

"I just had some free time before practice and wanted to surprise you," Dominic replied as he sat the flowers on her desk as she walked around it.

Walking up to him, "It's a pleasant surprise," she replied as she hugged him.

Pulling apart, "I see you are busy as ever," he joked as he looked over at her desk.

"You know a person's job is never done.

With Tazmin out on maternity leave, my load has doubled," Kamala said as she looked into his gray eyes, which seemed to look into her soul.

"How is Tazmin doing by the way?" he asked as he linked his fingers with hers.

"When I talked to her earlier, she was doing fine. She was ready to come home," she replied as she chuckled when she remembered how childish Tazmin sounded when she told her that the doctor wanted her to stay one more night in the hospital.

"I know how she feels, I don't like hospitals myself," Dominic stated.

"I think it has more to do with her trying to get back to work, then her having to stay in the hospital," Kamala suggested as he pulled her close to his body and hugged her.

"She'll be back here before she knows it. Before I leave, I wanted to know if you were free Friday night for dinner and then some dancing?" Dominic asked as he smiled down at her.

Trying to swallow the lump in her throat, "I can't this Friday, I already have plans. We can get together another night," Kamala suggested before she saw what looked like anger flash in his eyes and his grip on her body tightened.

Nodding his head as he stepped back from her and dropped his arms at his side. "It's alright, I'll call you later," he stated before starting to back up to the office door.

"I'm looking forward to it so I can see your famous dance moves," she joked but he didn't smile, he just nodded his head again as he turned around and headed for the door.

Kamala tried to smile even when it was the last thing, she felt like doing after she saw how hurt he was.

"Have fun Friday and I'll call you about next week," he replied before he opened the door and walked out with the door closing behind him.

With a heavy heart, Kamala walked around her desk and fell back into her chair. "What have I done?" she yelled as she replayed the look in Dominic's eyes when she told him she had plans.

"Kamala, are you alright?" Demetria asked as she entered the office followed by her sisters.

"We just saw Dominic leaving looking like he just lost his lunch money," Alondra joked causing Kamala to shake her head.

"I may have screwed up a great relationship," Kamala replied as she stood up and walked over to the window.

"What happened between you two?" Reyna asked as she and Demetria sat down in the chairs in front of Kamala's desk with Alondra and Rozlynn sitting on the matching sofa in the corner of the office.

"Dominic came by to surprise me with flowers, and then he asked me out Friday night for dinner and dancing," Kamala said.

"Okay, and what's wrong with that?" Demetria asked with a frown on her face.

"What's wrong with that is that I already have a date Friday night with Desmond," Kamala stated causing the ladies to smile.

"It's about damn time," Alondra yelled causing Kamala to shake her head again.

"I'm going to guess that Dominic didn't take the news well," Reyna stated causing Kamala to shake her head as guilt weighed heavily on her shoulders.

"That's the thing! I just said I have plans that night, but I could tell by the look in his eyes that he wasn't fooled," Kamala said as she turned in her seat.

"After this date with Desmond, you need to figure out who you want to be with. They both seem to be great guys to me," Demetria stated as she leaned back in her seat.

"I know, and I will figure this mess out, but enough about my drama, what do I owe for this visit?" Kamala asked as she looked around at her friends.

"We came to discuss Tazmin's Baby Shower. Since we couldn't give her one before she had the boys with the wedding and everything," Alondra said causing Kamala to smile as she thought about her friend and god babies.

"I thought we could have it in two months after we deal with our parents' death anniversary and plus it'll help lift her spirits,"
Reyna suggested.

Kamala knew that visiting their parents' graves would be hard on all of them, and maybe having the Shower after would be the best time.

"I agree with you, so let me handle the venue, and then we all can get together to handle the gifts," Kamala suggested just as the perfect place popped into her head.

"That sounds like a plan, let us know if we can help. I need to get going to my meeting that starts in about ten minutes," Alondra suggested as she stood up.

"Me too, thank you for helping with the Shower," Demetria stated as she also stood up.

"You don't have to thank me; that's what family do for each other," Kamala replied as the ladies walked toward her office door. Then they waved at her before walking out with the door closing behind them.

Then alone with her thoughts, *I have to get my life straightened out*, Kamala thought as she turned around and looked out the window again.

Chapter Fourteen

Stepping out of the shower, Kamala walked inside her closet to decide what to wear on her date with Desmond that night. Since they were having dinner at his place, she finally decided on her Jade colored abstract print maxi dress that had a unique cross over draped bodice and empire waist. Kamala also decided to add metallic wedge sandals and silver accessories hoping her look was casual enough. Laying her dress and jewelry on her bed, Kamala couldn't help, but wonder what Desmond had planned for them that evening.

After putting on lotion and her Lily scented fragrance, she then pulled on her dress. Kamala thought about the dream she had the night before, where she and Desmond made love under the stars on the beach. It seemed so real, and the way his hands moved so slowly over her body caused Kamala to moan as she tried to zip up her dress. Sitting down on her bed, she remembered how it felt to have him kissing and licking her sensitive spots such as her neck.

Then he lightly blew on it, which sent a shiver down her spine as she fastened the ankle straps of her sandals.

Taking a deep breath to calm down her racing heart rate, as she put on her silver necklace and chandelier earrings. Kamala knew she had to focus on getting through their dinner without any expectations, but she knew it was going to be hard when each night she was having erotic dreams about the man. Not to mention how she would feel if it was just two friends hanging out instead of a romantic dinner.

Walking over to her full-length mirror and running her fingers through her soft curls that framed her face and fell just past her shoulders. "Guess it's now or never to find out," she whispered before she turned and picked up her purse off her bed and headed downstairs.

Standing outside of the door of Desmond's penthouse, Kamala took a deep breath to calm the butterflies fluttering in her stomach. "Come on, you can do this!" she thought before she rang his doorbell.

Within seconds, the door opened with Desmond standing there, looking sexy as hell dressed in blue jeans and a navy V-neck sweater that did nothing to hide his muscles.

"Right on time!" he greeted as he opened the door wider and waved her inside.

"You know I hate being late," she replied smiling as she took in the grandeur of his home. "Desmond, this place is gorgeous," she continued as she walked into his living room that had an open and inviting feel.

The floors were tan marble that were gleaming as if they had just been polished; there was a magnificent view of Lake Michigan in the floor-to-ceiling windows that took her breath away. To her left was a spiral staircase leading up to the next level and to her right was a hallway leading somewhere else that was quirking her curiosity.

"Thank you for the compliment, and how about before we eat dinner, I'll give you the grand tour?" Desmond suggested as he held out his hand to her.

"I would like that," she replied as she placed her hand inside of his, and he gently pulled her down the hallway.

As Desmond showed her his home, Kamala was blown away. It had a wraparound terrace, private basketball and squash courts, large hot tub, and three saltwater aquariums. There was one in the living room, one in the main hallway, and one in the man cave.

His bedroom was what caught her attention because on the floor was black onyx marble and the area around his king size bed's headboard was a wall of Onyx Marble as a backdrop. Then with the dark and masculine accessories it just screamed romance. Not to mention the view of the city at your feet as you lay in bed, to relax you after a long day at work.

Walking down the stairs heading back into the living room, "Desmond, you have got to give me your decorator's phone number," Kamala suggested as they finally arrived back in the living room.

"You already have it," he replied as he started caressing her hand with his thumb drawing a frown on her face.

"Riley decorated your house?" she asked as she looked up at him.

"No, I decorated my house with the help of my sister and Mrs. London," he replied smiling.

"Forgive me for jumping to conclusions. I just assumed that since she was your girlfriend that she might have helped you," she confessed as she pulled her hand back and walked over to his window to enjoy the view.

She felt him walk over to her causing her to look up at him, "Kamala, I ended my relationship with Riley because we weren't meant to be together. I also asked you to come here, because I want to get to know you and spend time with you," he confessed causing a shiver to go down her spine.

Turning around to face him and give him her full attention, "Why now? We've known each other for years," she asked, not sure if she wanted to know his answer.

Gently grabbing her hand again, "How about we start eating dinner before it gets cold. Then I can tell you everything?" he asked as he laced their fingers together, and she drew in a shaky breath before nodding her head.

Following him into the dining room, she noticed the table was set with elegant onyx
China, and gleaming silverware.

"Desmond, this is a beautiful setting," she said as he pulled out her chair and she sat down.

"It's my pleasure, but I can't take all the credit because Mrs. London cooked the dinner. I just set the table," he replied smiling as he sat down in the chair to her left.

"If Mrs. London cooked the food, then I know it's going to be great," Kamala said as she placed her napkin in her lap.

"If you liked her cooking, then I will definitely cook for you since I learned from her and my mom," Desmond replied as he also put his napkin in his lap.

"Yes, you will, if you can make your mother's special ribs and potato salad," Kamala joked smiling.

She remembered all the times during college where she, Desmond, and Tazmin went to his parents' house for dinner. They had such an enjoyable time as they ate great food while they talked and joked around together.

Chuckling, "As a matter of fact, I'm making some for dinner at my sister's house tomorrow night. You are welcome to come if you want to join us," he suggested causing her to sigh at the thought of those ribs.

Smiling, "I may take you up on that offer," she replied.

"You're more than welcome to come, and I'm sure the gang would love to see you. Let's eat before the food gets cold," he suggested as he lifted the silver cover off his plate with her doing the same.

A tantalizing scent hit her nose, causing her to look down at the marinated sliced strip steak with mashed potatoes and gravy, and fresh spinach.

"How do you like our menu for tonight?" he asked as he started to cut up his steak.

"You know I love Mrs. London's cooking. Especially her homemade chicken noodle soup," Kamala replied before taking the first bite of her steak, which caused her to close her eyes and moan as she's savored the amazing taste and tenderness.

When she opened her eyes, she found Desmond watching her with such interest. "Why are you looking at me like that? This food is so good," she asked before tasting the potatoes next.

"If I can get that reaction out of you more often, then I'll make sure Mrs. London cooks for you every day," he stated as he winked at her causing her to blush.

"There you go with that sly tongue of yours," she stated as she continued to enjoy her amazing food.

"Kamala, I'm only speaking the truth. Plus, I bet you didn't know that I had a crush on you for years?" Desmond asked causing her to stop chewing and look at him like he was crazy.

"Stop playing! During college, you had a different girl every week. So there was no way you would have noticed me back then," Kamala replied before continuing to eat.

"There weren't as many girls as you think. The few that I did date didn't last long because they couldn't compare to you," he revealed causing her hands to start shaking as she put her fork down on her plate.

"If that's the case, why didn't you ever say anything to me?" she asked as she narrowed her eyes at him.

"With my so-called playboy ways and reputation would you have believed me?" he asked as he narrowed his eyes at her.

Taking a deep breath, and shaking her head, "Probably not, but I guess we both were hiding things back then," she replied as she picked up her fork and finished the last of the food.

"And what were you hiding back then?" he asked as he also finished his food.

Drawing in a shaky breath and looking into his eyes, "All these years, you never guessed that I had a crush on you?"

she asked. Kamala watched as his eyes widened, and then they both put their forks down on their plates.

"Now, I don't believe that! Plus, you were dating that guy in Miami," he replied causing guilt to weigh heavily on her shoulders as she thought about Dominic.

"I ended things with him because long distance relationships don't work out. Plus, I really did have a crush on you then, but I knew that you didn't like girls that weren't cheerleaders," she replied as she pushed her plate away. Then she remembered all the nights she had cried herself to sleep because he never took the time to notice her.

"Kamala, you were and still are the most beautiful woman I've ever known," he confessed as he gently grabbed her hand and started to caress it with his thumb.

"Thank you for saying that, but it's not going to stop me from kicking your butt in a game of pool," she joked as she looked everywhere, but at him. While she processed what he had just confessed to her, she could feel her heart racing in her chest.

"I'm just speaking the truth! As for that game, let's head to the game room so I can beat you really fast," he said as he stood up and pulled her behind him out of the dining room.

Following him out of the dining room, Kamala was battling with the news that they both had crushes on each other all that time. She didn't know what he wanted her to do with that information.

"So how does it feel to lose to me again?" Kamala joked as she laid her pool stick on the table after hitting the eight-ball in the corner pocket.

"If I get to lose to someone as beautiful as you then I'm fine," he replied as he laid his stick on the table next to hers and slowly walked over to her.

"Is that so, Mr. Flemings?" she asked as he stood in front of her with her back pressed against the pool table.

The intense look in his eyes, as he looked down at her, had her stomach fluttering as she took shallow breaths to calm her racing heart.

Slowly caressing her cheek with the back of his hand, "That is definitely right! Right now, I want to do something I've wanted to do for nine years," he whispered as he closed the distance between them.

Looking into his eyes, "And what might that be?" she gasped as he wrapped his arms around her waist and pulled her closer to his body. Being so close she could smell his cologne, and she realized it was Guilty by Gucci.

Close enough that they were sharing air, "This!" he whispered before his lips touched hers, causing them both to moan.

His taste was addictive, as Kamala felt she couldn't get enough of him as she wrapped her arms around his neck and pulled him closer. The feel of his velvet tongue caressing hers was almost her undoing. Being in his arms at that moment was better than all the dreams she had been having for the past few weeks. As he started to caress her back, Kamala released a moan as shockwaves went straight to her womanhood.

Deepening their kiss, Kamala gasped when she felt him lift her up onto the edge of the pool table before he moved between her legs. Pressing closer to him as her hands caressed his chest earning her a groan from him as he nibbled at her bottom lip. She could feel his desire radiating from his body, causing her to moan as his rigid member that was concealed by his jeans pressed against her center.

Slowly, she eased her hands down his chest, loving the hardness of his muscles as they flexed under her touch. When she reached the hem of his shirt, she quickly lifted it over his head, revealing the mouthwatering view of his eight pack abs that had her panting. Pulling him back to her, Kamala felt him slowly pull down the shoulder straps of her dress, revealing her black strapless bra. He had groaned at the sight before he began placing love bites on her shoulder as he skillfully unfastened her bra.

Letting her head fall back, as she pushed her aching breasts into his hands after he removed her bra. The electric current flowing through her body, Kamala felt so delirious with need, and it only intensified when his hot mouth latched onto her hard and sensitive nipple. She arched her back as she put her hands into his silky dreads and pulled his head closer to her breasts.

Continuing to nibble on her nipples, Kamala realized his hand were slowly easing her dress up her legs when the cool air in the room hit her hot skin causing her to sigh.

"Please Desmond!" she moaned as his hand glided closer to her aching womanhood. Kamala had to fight the urge to squeeze her legs together as the aching intensified.

Pulling back from his juicy lips and looking into his passion filled eyes as she gasps for air, Kamala slowly ran her hands down his chest and abs before she came to the edge of his jeans. Deciding to have a little fun, she let her hand glide down over his hard member that was perfectly outlined in his jeans.

She earned a groan from him as he gripped her thighs, and he stepped closer to her, opening her legs wider. Still looking into Desmond's eyes that seemed to narrow at her, she slowly ran her hand back up over his member. She enjoyed the feel of his rigid member and the material of the jeans against her skin.

Licking her lips, she slowly unfastened his jeans as she saw the fire in his eyes intensify as his hands caressed her thighs causing her to moan. While pulling the zipper down, and hearing that sound, it sent a current through her body, causing her to squeeze her legs around him. Needing to touch him, Kamala slowly pushed his jeans and boxers down his legs, causing his member to spring out and her to gasp. Wrapping her hand around his hard and long member, Kamala couldn't help licking her lips again as she thought about all the pleasure they were about to experience.

Desmond must have read her mind, as his hand slid between her legs and his lips came down on hers causing her to moan. The force of his lips pressing against hers as his tongue opened her lips and met hers, Kamala was almost at her breaking point as the pressure in her stomach intensified. Needing more, she wrapped her legs around his hips as his hand moved her thong aside and started to manipulate her sensitive folds causing her to gasp.

Panting as their kiss became wild and exotic, her need to have him inside of her almost drove her insane. Getting the message, Desmond pulled her closer to the edge of the table with one of her legs over his arm. He slowly rubbed his member against her center, earning a moan from her as a shutter rocked her entire body. When he slowly entered her opening, they both groaned, and Kamala closed her eyes as her womanhood had started pulsating uncontrollably causing her to throw her head back.

Between the mesmerizing feel of his hard member going in and out of her and the magical feel of his fingers as they massaged her extremely sensitive clit, Kamala thought her mind was going to short-circuit. When his pace started to pick up, Kamala held onto his strong shoulders as she started to match his thrust with her own causing them to moan. The pulsing of her womanhood, and the pressure building it her core, Kamala needed more as she deepened their kiss as her hands threaded through his dreads.

"Desmond!" she screamed as she free fell over her orgasmic cliff, causing her to gasp as her hold tightened on him as he continued to pound into her.

Shockwaves racing through her body, Desmond continued his assault on her senses as he applied more pressure to her clit, causing her to scream as she threw her head back again.

"That's it baby!" he whispered as he grabbed both of her butt cheeks and pulled her to him as his pace increased.

As a pressure started to build again, Kamala didn't know how much more pleasure she could take. Meeting his thrusts and losing all her restraints, Kamala let her body enjoy all the sensations flowing through her just as she heard him release a loud groan and his body stiffened. Still thrusting down on his member, Kamala felt her release crashing down on her, causing her to scream. Feeling him slowly moving inside of her, Kamala realize that her dreams couldn't compare to the real thing.

With her heart racing and gasping for air, "Damn!" she whispered as he gently pulled out of her and pulled his boxers and jeans up.

"My thoughts exactly," he whispered before he kissed her so slowly and tenderly causing her to moan.

Pulling back and looking up into his intense eyes, Kamala knew that after she had finally sampled the erotic pleasure that he could give her, she became determined to experience more. Then she pulled him to her with her legs wrapped around his waist and her hands running through his dreads.

Chapter Fifteen

Feeling the sun on her face, Kamala opened her eyes, and she started to panic when she didn't recognize where she was. Then it dawned on her that she was still at Desmond's place, as everything from the night before came rushing back to her causing a blush to rise in her cheeks.

She remembered all the naughty things they had done to each other the night before through to the next morning, before falling asleep in each other's arms. Looking to her left, Kamala found Desmond looking handsome as ever as he slept so peacefully. Thinking of all the sensational things he did to her body the night before, Kamala slowly turned on her side and started to run her hand down his cheek before she started to kiss his neck.

All too soon, his arms pulled her onto his chest, "If I can wake up like this every morning, I may never let you leave," he whispered. Kamala's womanhood started throbbing at the deepness of his voice as it flowed through her body.

Kissing him softly, "Is that a promise?" she asked smiling.

Kissing her passionately until they both were moaning and gasping for air as they pulled apart, "It most definitely is," he replied smiling. Then he ran his hand down her back causing a shiver to run down her spine.

Looking into his eyes, "I'm so glad we finally got everything out in the open," she said as she looked down at him while she leaned on his chest.

"Kamala, last night was the best night of my life. I just can't get over that we both had feeling for each other, and it took all these years for me to finally ask you out on a date. I just hope that you give us a chance to get to the point where we are with each other for forever," he confessed. Hearing his words brought a smile to her face as she released the breath, she had been holding.

Slowly straddling his waist, Kamala put her hands on his pillow by his head with their naked chest pressed against each other. "Desmond, last night meant a lot to me too, I want to see where this goes also," she whispered. Then she kissed him, and his arms closed around her and pulled her closer to his body.

Loving his taste as their tongues caressed, Kamala realized that she was quickly becoming addicted to Desmond. She hoped that she was making the right choice, but if not, she was going to enjoy her time with him while it lasted, starting with making love with him again.

Taking a deep breath as he looked down at the gorgeous woman lying on his chest, Desmond couldn't help the smile that lit up his face. Kamala had somehow filled the empty hole in his heart that was caused by losing his parents and all the bad relationships he had been in over the years. Just seeing her smile or hearing her sensual voice caused his body to go haywire with need. Running his hand down her back, caused her to moan in her sleep, which made him realize how addictive he was to that woman.

In all those years, he had known her and had a crush on her, couldn't compare to the love he felt for her at that moment. Kissing her forehead and brushing her soft hair out of her eyes, Desmond couldn't get over how lucky he was to have her in his life finally. He was determined to do everything in his power not to fuck it up. Kissing her softly on her lips, Desmond slowly eased out of the bed, after deciding he was going to show her just how much he cherished her, by starting with breakfast in bed.

Setting the tray full of bacon, eggs, toast, and orange juice on his nightstand, Desmond slowly eased back into bed and started placing soft kisses on her back. Soon he earned a moan from her that set his insides on fire. When she finally opened her eyes smiling, "Good morning beautiful," he greeted as she then rolled over on her back giving him a tantalizing view of her sexy naked body.

"Good morning handsome," Kamala moaned as he started caressing her breasts while he felt his manhood respond to the erotic sound.

"I made you breakfast, and I have a question to ask you," he replied as he sat with his back against the headboard.

Sitting beside him and pulling the sheet over her body, "Thank you for breakfast, and what did you want to ask me?" she asked as he placed the tray on her lap.

"Since I'm fixing my mom's famous ribs that you love so much, I was wondering if you still wanted to come to dinner at my sister's house with me today?" he asked just as she placed a piece of bacon at his lips.

Looking into her beautiful eyes, as he slowly drew her fingers into his mouth and licked them before she pulled them back. Desmond could see the fire burning in her eyes and realized it wasn't just him.

"I would love to go with you! Plus, you know I can't resist those ribs," she joked as she continued to eat and feed him at the same time.

"Since that's settled, we still have a few hours to waste. So what do you suggest we do with all that time?" he asked just before he kissed her, earning him another moan as she put her arms around his neck.

"How about we let nature take its course," she whispered before kissing him and stealing his breath.

When they pulled apart gasping for air, Desmond quickly moved the tray back to his nightstand, causing Kamala to chuckle at his eagerness before she pulled him on top of her as she kissed him. Feeling her soft lips against his, Desmond realized he could never get enough of her.

Pulling up to his sister's five-bedroom home and cutting off his SUV, Desmond looked over at the woman who had held his heart in her hands for so many years. He was so glad that they had finally come together. Kamala was dressed in a teal top that had a design that crossed over her voluptuous breast causing his mouth to water.

She also had on black capris that showed her curvy butt and legs perfectly making him want to cancel dinner and take her back to his penthouse. Looking down at his black jeans and red V-neck sweater, Desmond didn't know if he should have changed into something a little dressier.

"Desmond, are we going to stay in the car with you undressing me with your eyes, or are we going inside?" Kamala asked as she ran her hand slowly up his leg.

Smiling, "If I had my way we would still be at my place," he replied before leaning over and kissing her juicy lips, before proceeding to climb out of his car.

Walking around the car to the passenger door and open it, "Right this way," he joked as he offered her his hand. Desmond enjoyed the view of her body moving so fluently as she climbed out of his car and into his waiting arms.

"I could definitely get used to this," he whispered before kissing Kamala, savoring the fullness of her lips and the sweet taste as their tongues caressed each other.

Pulling apart, and needing to breathe, "Me too, but right now we need to stop before the neighbors called the cops on us for indecent exposure," she joked causing him to chuckle.

Shaking his head, and linking their fingers together, Desmond led her to the front door, where he pushed the doorbell. Looking at each other smiling, he then heard the door open within seconds. When he looked up, he saw Kingsley standing there grinning at them like she had lost her mind, causing him to clear his throat.

"I'm sorry, come on in," Kingsley greeted as she waved them inside while still grinning like a fool.

Shaking his head, he led Kamala into the living room where Adam and Ryder were watching a basketball game.

"What's up guys?" Desmond greeted as Ryder and Adam stood up grinning like fools also causing Desmond to frown as he looked around at his family.

"Hey, Bro and Kamala!" Ryder greeted as he bumped fist with Desmond and hugged
Kamala.

"Hi Ryder and Adam, long time no see," Kamala replied as she hugged Adam next just as Kingsley walked into the room smiling.

"It sure is! I've been telling my big head brother to bring you by," Ryder replied to causing Kamala to chuckle as

Desmond put his arm around her and led her over to the suede love seat and sat down.

After sitting down and looking at Kamala, she looked over at him with desire in her eyes, and it took everything in him not to kiss her senseless. She must have picked up on his thoughts because she blushed and winked as she gently squeezed his hand as it lay in her lap.

Smiling like an idiot, Desmond looked over at his family to find them watching him like a hawk.

Not wanting to make Kamala uncomfortable, "Guys, why don't you help me get the food out of my car," he suggested. Then he kissed Kamala quickly and then led the guys out of the room.

The moment they stepped outside, and the door was closed, "Why are you guys smiling at us like that?" Desmond demanded as he hit the unlock button on his keychain.

Chuckling, "Man, we were just glad that you finally got your shit together. Then finally got with a woman that genuinely loves you," Ryder replied as he opened the hatchback of the SUV, where all the containers of food were.

"I agree with Ryder because your sister and I could tell that Kamala loved you from the beginning, but you were walking around with blinders on your eyes. I was beginning to worry about your sister attacking you for being so slow, "Adam joked causing the guys to chuckle.

"I don't know what took me so long to own up to my feelings for her. Plus, I had no idea that she had any romantic feelings for me," Desmond replied causing his brothers to shake their heads.

"Come on man! Over the years, you never wondered why she always stood by your side for the good and bad times, or the way she looked at you sometimes?" Adam asked as he picked up the containers of ribs and collards.

"Or the way she would check on you daily or how she went out of her way for your birthday or holidays?" Ryder asked as he picked up the macaroni and cheese and potato salad.

Picking up the containers of broccoli and cheese casserole and a strawberry cheesecake, "I don't know why I didn't notice it all these years. Now that I finally have her in my life, I'm going to make sure to cherish her," Desmond replied before closing the hatchback.

"You better or you will have to deal with us and you know how crazy Kingsley is," Ryder joked causing the guys to chuckle as they walked back into the house.

"I'm not joking, Desmond used to torture Ryder. I'll never forget when Desmond shaved Ryder's eyebrows off,"

Kingsley joked causing the group to laugh except Ryder, who was glaring at Desmond.

"That's just wrong!" Kamala said as she lightly hit Desmond's arm as she continued to laugh.

"Hey, in my defense I didn't want to share my parents' and sister's attention. Plus, they spoiled me, so it is their fault," Desmond replied causing Kingsley to throw a napkin at him.

After dinner, and as they sat at the dinner table, Desmond realize how good it felt to have his family and the woman he loved all together.

"I will admit that we did spoil him, and he could do no wrong in our eyes. So you could say that we created a monster," Kingsley stated smiling.

"My feelings for Ryder changed when he turned four years old and someone at a playground had punched him and pushed him down on the ground making him cry. After seeing him hurt like that, I beat the brakes off that boy and took Ryder home to get his knee checked out. Since then we've been thick as thieves," Desmond confessed as he looked over at his brother, and they smiled at each other.

"I remember that day because you beat up Danny Freeman and his friends. After that, whenever they saw me coming, they would run the other way," Ryder added causing the group to chuckle.

"Hey, what are brothers for?" Desmond asked.

"Listening to you guys, makes me wish I had siblings growing up," Kamala stated, and when Desmond looked over at her, he could see the sadness in her eyes.

Putting his arm around her, "Being around this crowd, you'll be glad you were an only child," he joked causing her to smile again.

"I doubt it! After meeting Tazmin and her family, and them welcoming me into their family, I don't know what I would do without them in my life," she replied. Then she intertwined her fingers with Desmond's, and he enjoyed the closeness that they were sharing.

"Well, now you are a part of our family too," Kingsley replied bringing a smile to Desmond's face as he vowed to do everything in his power to keep his family together.

Chapter Sixteen

"Girl, I don't know what I would do without Adonis! Between the middle of the night feedings and the diaper changes, I wouldn't get any rest or have any hair left after pulling it out. If it wasn't for him helping out," Tazmin joked as they sat in the living room of Tazmin and Adonis's six-bedroom penthouse. Kamala was holding Hunter, who was looking up at her smiling as she made funny faces at him.

"How many times do they wake up each night?" Kamala asked just as Hunter squealed in excitement, bring a smile to her face.

"It seems as soon as one goes to sleep; the other one wakes up. Like now, Hunter is awake, but when he takes his nap, Hayden will wake up," Tazmin replied as they both looked over at Hayden, who was asleep in his playpen.

"I can't imagine having to deal with one newborn, and here you are with two," Kamala stated as she looked down at Hunter.

He was watching her as if she was the strangest thing he had ever seen.

"Even with the late-night feedings and diaper changes, it's all worth it. When I look into their cute faces and see gleams of me and Adonis, it brightens my day," Tazmin replied as she looked at her babies.

"Hopefully one day I will have one of my own," Kamala said as she lightly caressed Hunter's cheek, earning her another squeal, which caused her and Tazmin to chuckle.

"Since we are on that subject, when can I expect you and Desmond to have my god babies?" Tazmin asked causing Kamala to turn her head toward her so fast she almost got whiplash, as Tazmin started laughing.

Shaking her head, "Girl, we are a long way from that. Plus, I'm confused about how to handle Dominic, now that I'm with Desmond," Kamala replied as Hunter yawned, and she started to gently rock him.

"What's going on with Dominic?" Tazmin asked with a frown on her face.

"When he came to my office last week, and I told him that I couldn't go to dinner with him because I already had plans. I could see the anger in his eyes, and it sent a chill down my spine," Kamala replied causing Tazmin to narrow her eyes.

"Did he say anything out of the way to you?" Tazmin asked in a hard tone.

Shaking her head, "No, he didn't, but I could tell he was trying to hide his anger. He's supposed to call me about having dinner together this week. Now that Desmond has entered the picture, I know that I have to end things with Dominic," Kamala confessed as she looked down and realized Hunter had fallen asleep.

"Kamala, the best thing to do is to end things with Dominic before things get worse. If you need me there for support, I'll be there," Tazmin suggested as she stood up, walked over to Kamala, and picked up Hunter before laying him down in his playpen.

Shaking her head, "No, I need to handle this alone, but I'll let you know if I need backup," Kamala joked causing Tazmin to chuckle. Kamala remembered all the times they had joined together to handle ex-boyfriends.

Looking at her friend and sister, "Onto a more important topic, are you ready for the anniversary coming up?" Kamala asked as she watched the smile fall from Tazmin's face.

"You would think after all these years that going to their graves each year would get easier, but it doesn't," Tazmin confessed as a tear ran down her cheek. Kamala moved to the other sofa beside Tazmin as she offered her a tissue.

"There isn't a timetable on the grieving process, plus you will never forget the hell you all went through, but as the years go by, it does get easier to deal with. With my mom's death, I'm still dealing with it, so I can't imagine what you are going through," Kamala whispered as she hugged Tazmin.

"It does get easier, but it still hurts, and now that day is rapidly approaching again. This year, we all are meeting here, and then we are going to the gravesite together.

Afterward, we will come back here for dinner to celebrate our parents life and legacy," Tazmin revealed as tears rolled down her cheek. Kamala felt her tears on her cheek, which she tried to wipe away.

"And as you know, I will be there for you guys the whole time," Kamala whispered as they hugged again before pulling apart and chuckling at the sight of their running mascara.

"We look a mess," Tazmin joked as they tried to fix each other's makeup.

"Are you two alright?" Adonis asked as he and Desmond walked into the living room.

Standing up smiling, "We are fine! We just got a little emotional as we talked about the anniversary," Tazmin replied as she walked into Adonis's arms and hugged him.

Looking up, Kamala saw Desmond looking at her with a frown on his face, causing her to beckon him with her finger. When he sat down beside her with his arm around her shoulders, she kissed him. Savoring his minty taste, Kamala couldn't get enough, causing her to pull back before she got carried away.

"Are you sure you're alright?" Desmond asked after they pulled apart with the frown still on his face.

"Yes, I'm fine! What have you two been up too?" Kamala asked as Adonis and Tazmin sat on the sofa across from them.

"We were at the studio, laying versus down on one of the songs for Adonis's new album," Desmond replied as he linked his fingers with hers.

"Were you able to get it finished?" Tazmin asked as she looked at Adonis and Desmond.

"You know how we do it! It was a slam dunk. Plus, we started on the next track before calling it quits for the day," Adonis replied causing the group to chuckle. "Yeah, I know how you two do, and I'm proud of your progress," Tazmin replied before she kissed Adonis.

Taking that as their cue to leave, "As much fun as this is, I have an early start tomorrow. So we are going to leave you two lovebirds alone," Kamala stated as she looked over at Desmond, and then they both stood up.

"You don't have to leave so soon," Tazmin said as she and Adonis also stood up.

"Yes, we do, unlike you, I have a ton of reports to go through and three meetings with vendors and lawyers tomorrow," Kamala replied as she hugged Tazmin and Adonis.

"Plus, I have to add a few changes to Godric's album before completing Adonis's tracks," Desmond added as he hugged Tazmin next.

"Alright guys, we'll see you later and drive carefully," Tazmin replied smiling as they walked to the front door.

"And I'll see you at the studio tomorrow," Adonis added as he bumped his fist against Desmond's.

"Alright, I'll be there, and we'll drive carefully," Desmond replied before they walked out of the door.

As soon as the door closed behind them, Desmond pulled Kamala into his arms, "I have missed you all day," Desmond whispered causing her womanhood with throb with need as her breath became labored.

"I know how you feel. So let's go to my place and show each other how much," she replied before she closed the distance between them and kissed him with all the pent-up emotions flooding her body. Both of them were so wrapped up in their passion when both of them moaned.

Pulling apart with the need to air, "What are we waiting for?" Desmond asked if he led her to the elevator.

Looking over at Desmond and seeing the desire that she knew was mirrored in her eyes, Kamala couldn't wait to get home.

When Kamala opened her front door, she was greeted by a dozen red roses, causing her to frown. Then she started to panic when she realized they were from Dominic.

Looking over Desmond, who was looking at her and then over at the roses, "We need to talk," she stated as she walked over to the beautiful roses and pulled the card off and read it,

Beautiful flowers for a beautiful woman, Dominic.

Taking a deep breath, Kamala led Desmond into her living room, where she walked over to the window to get her thoughts together.

"Kamala, what's going on here?" Desmond asked as he stood beside her.

"Do you remember the night the ladies and I went to Club Heat to see Malik perform?" she asked as her heart rate started to race.

"Yes, I do, what does that have to do with who sent you those roses?" Desmond asked as he put his hands in his jean pockets.

"While we were there, I ran into Dominic Taylor, my high school sweetheart. He also happened to be the guy I was dating when I started college," she replied before she saw the shocked expression on his face.

"You dated The Dominic Taylor of the Chicago Bears?" he asked before releasing a deep breath.

"Yes, that night we exchanged numbers and even had a few dinner dates since then. Which is why I couldn't go out with you when you asked me before," she confessed.

She wanted to wipe away the hurt that she saw development in his eyes.

"Do you have feelings for this guy?" Desmond asked, causing her heart to ache from the pain she heard in his voice that she had caused.

"In high school and at the beginning of college, yes, I did love him, but I knew long distance relationship didn't work out, so I ended things with him. Plus, after meeting you, my feelings toward him changed. Then I figured you would never see me that way after you decided to date the cheerleader type. So when he came back into town, I figured it was a sign to stop hoping you would notice me and love me back. So I decided to move on with my life," Kamala revealed as she felt tears flood her eyes.

Turning away from Desmond as her tears rolled down her cheek, Kamala didn't know how she got herself into that situation. At the end of the day, she may lose the only man she had ever truly loved. Wiping her cheek and waiting for him to end whatever their relationship was, Kamala could feel her heart breaking into a million pieces.

Hearing him sigh before he placed his hand under her chin and turning her around to look at him, "Kamala, I'm not upset with you for moving on with your life. I'm just upset with myself for taking so long to tell you that I love you. If we had been honest with each other, we could have avoided years of heartache," he confessed before he pulled her into his arms, and she realized he had just said he loved her for the first time.

Wiping her cheek as she looked up at him, "Where do we go from here? Do you want a relationship with me or are we just going to be friends with benefits?" Kamala asked before holding her breath as she waited for his answer.

Smiling, "Baby, I love you with everything in me, and I have for years. So, yes I want a relationship with you and only you," he whispered before kissing her softly on her lips and then pulled back and looked into her eyes.

Excitement rushed through her body as she put her arms around his neck, "I love you too, and I want to be in a relationship with you also," she whispered. Then she pulled his head down and kissed him with all the love and passion she felt for him.

The strength and power he exemplified caused her desire to engulf inside of her. Her need for him had her delirious as she reached for the hem of his sweater and pulled it over his head, before kissing him again. Their kiss was full of desire causing her heart rate to accelerate as she ran her hands down his chest earning a groan from him. Desmond quickly removed her top and tossed it on the floor next to his before pulling her back into his arms and kissing her with such force.

The heat of his skin next to hers was exhilarating. When he unfastened her red lace bra and threw it on the floor, Kamala's knees grew weak when he's hot mouth lavished her breasts with kisses. Panting and running her hands through his dreads, Kamala didn't know if she could stand much more. Then she gasped when her hot skin was pressed back against the cold glass of the window. While Desmond kissed his way down her body as he unfastened her pants, before pushing them down her legs to reveal her matching red lace thong.

Watching his eyes feast on the sight of her underwear and hearing the sound of him groaning with need and desire quickly brought a smile to her face. Wrapped up in her own sexual haze, she continued to enjoy the feel of his skin against her hands. Feeling the force of his muscles flexing under her touch, Kamala enjoying his reaction to her caresses when he released a deep moan. Then he lifted one of her legs over his shoulders as he continued to lavish her skin with kisses, Kamala could feel the adrenaline rushing through her veins as she waited to see what he would do next.

First, she was nervous that she was going to fall, and then all her thoughts flew out of her mind whcn his mouth latched onto her sensitive clit causing her to scream out. The sensations flowing through her body from head to toe and the feel of his strong arms holding her into place,

Kamala felt like she was putty in Desmond's hands. Needing more, Kamala's grip on his hair tightened as he licked and sucked on her womanhood until she was screaming out his name.

Tension building in her core and the pulses vibrating to her womanhood, as her head started to thrash back and forth on the glass window, Kamala's world exploded, "Desmond!" she screamed as a shudder wracked her body causing her to gasp.

Clinging to his shoulders, as numerous waves of ecstasy passed through her body, Kamala realize Desmond was slowly standing up. Pulling his mouth to hers and tasting her essence on his lips seemed to set her blood on fire as their tongues battled for dominance, which he quickly won. Running her hands down his back as both of his hands grabbed her butt and pulled her closer to his rigid member causing her to moan. Then she realized that he had released his member from his jeans as it rubbed against her stomach.

Loving the silky feel of his member as it glided across her skin caused a shutter to rush through her body. Kamala thought she was going to go out of her mind if she didn't feel him inside of her soon, "Desmond please!" she moaned.

Gasping as he lifted her into his arms, "Let's take this to a more comfortable setting," he whispered as he walked toward her bedroom.

Putting her arms around his neck and her legs around his waist, "You must have read my mind," she replied. Then she started to kiss his neck causing him to groan as his hold around her waist tightened.

Hearing the sound of his groan seemed to vibrate through her body, stealing her breath away, and she couldn't wait to see what he did next.

Entering her bedroom, Desmond gently laid her down on her bed before he stepped back and started to undress. Watching as he stepped out of his jeans, Kamala moved into the center of her king size bed on her back. She was enjoying the strip show he was performing causing her to moan at the sight of his long and hard member as he walked back to the bed. She quickly removed her thong and tossed it on the floor and saw his eyes light up with fire when she opened her legs giving him the perfect view of her throbbing womanhood. Seeing the fire in his eyes, caused the throbbing in her womanhood to intensify making her release a loud gasp and cover her center hoping to lessen the intensity.

So wrapped up in the sensations flooding her body, Kamala hadn't noticed that Desmond had joined her on the bed until he gently removed her hand and kissed each of her fingers. Then he laid between her legs. His kisses were so gentle and loving it brought tears to her eyes.

Looking into her eyes, "I love you so much," he whispered before he kissed her with such force, it stole her breath away. Putting her arms around his neck, and pulling him closer to her body, she felt his hard member pressing against her pelvis. Gasping as their kiss deepened, and their tongues battled for dominance, Kamala's need to feel him inside of her dominated her every thought. Grinded her pelvis against his member, caused him to groan as his hold onto her tighter.

When he pulled back, so that they could get some much-needed air, and they looked into each other's eyes, all she saw was love, and she knew that she needed him as much as she needed the air filling her lungs at that moment. As she pulled his lips back to hers, she felt his hand glide down her stomach, to her aching womanhood, causing her to gasp. Heart racing and her body feeling as if it's on fire, as he manipulated her folds and sensitive clit, Kamala's core felt so tightly wound, that it was about to snap.

When his slowly eased his member, into her, they both gasped as she tightened her arms around his neck. Loving how full she felt as he filled her to capacity, Kamala started to run her nails down his back causing him to moan as he threw his head back and picked up his pace. His thrust were so powerful, she could hear her headboard banging against the wall.

Looking up into his eyes, and when he looked down at her, Kamala wanted him to experience the multitude of pleasure she was. So she started to meet his thrust, causing a shudder to pass through his body as she continued to rake her nails down his back.

Grinding their pelvis, Kamala's head started to thrash back and forth as the pressure in her core and the aching in her womanhood reached its breaking point causing her to scream. Enjoying the ecstasy flowing through her body, Kamala dug her nails into his back as she arched her back off of the bed. With stars flashing before her eyes and her gasping for air, Kamala heard Desmond release a deep groan that vibrated through his chest as his paces started to slow down. When he closed the distance between their hot and sweat covered bodies, Kamala moaned again as she put her arms around his neck. Feeling his juicy lips against hers, Kamala wrapped her legs around him to pull him closer to her body, not wanting to let him go.

Gasping, "You do know that you have created a monster, and I may never let you leave this bed," she whispered causing him to chuckle as he looked down into her eyes. "Is that so?" he asked as he started to move his still hard member in and out of her very slowly causing her to moan. "What would you say if I said that I want to stay in this bed and you for the rest of my life?" he continued before he lowered his head and pulled her sensitive nipple into his mouth. He stopped anything she was about to say because all she could do was close her eyes as her moans flowed from her mouth.

Giving herself over to Desmond and his magical touch, Kamala knew she would give him anything he asked for if he kept making her feel like that.

Chapter Seventeen

Two weeks later as she sat in her office, Kamala thought about how her relationship with Desmond had blossomed. They had become inseparable and had even become even closer friends than before. Being with Desmond, seemed as if her life had light and purpose. With one look or smile, her day seems to get better.

In the little time they had been together, Desmond had spoiled her with breakfast in bed, nights full of passion and had cemented his place in her heart. Looking on her desk at the picture of him, Adonis, Tazmin, and herself at Tazmin and Adonis's wedding, she hoped that they would continue to progress to a lasting relationship. She also knew it was too early to tell.

Then she thought about the one hurdle in their way, Dominic. He was still sending her flowers and gifts, and when she tried to call him to discuss their situation, she kept getting his voicemail. It was as if he was avoiding her, but she couldn't understand why. She decided to try and call him again, she picked up her office phone and dialed his cell phone number. As it started to ring, Kamala tried to figure out what she was going to say when his voicemail picked up again. Sighing as she ended the call, Kamala knew that she had to figure out a way to reach Dominic very soon.

Just as she was dialing his home phone number, someone knocked on her office door, causing her to frown because she didn't have any meeting scheduled at that time.

"Come in!" she yelled as she ended the call she was making.

Then Dominic walked into her office smiling with more flowers.

"Hello beautiful," he greeted as he walked further into office after shutting the door.

"Hello yourself! I was just calling you as a matter of fact," she replied as she stood up and hugged him.

"That means I have perfect timing," he stated as he sat down in the chair in front of her desk while she returned to her office chair.

"Yes, it does, because I need to talk to you about something," she said as she began to worry about how he was going to react to her news.

"How about we go to dinner tonight and talk about it then since I need to be getting to practice?" he asked as he jumped up.

"Dominic, I can't go to dinner with you because I'm involved with someone else," she blurted out. Kamala saw him pause, and she could see the anger in his eyes again before he quickly covered it up with a fake smile that didn't reach his eyes.

"Kamala, I understand someone else is in the picture, but I can't lose you again. This time I will fight for us," he confessed as he walked backward toward her door.

"There is nothing you can do to change my mind. So let's just agree to be friends," she suggested as she watched him put his hand on the door handle and open the door.

"Kamala, I will never give up on us again. So be ready for me to fight for you this time," he confessed before walking out of her office before she could respond.

Still looking at her door, "What in the hell just happened?" she asked as she shook her head and thought about their whole conversation.

"This is crazy!" she yelled as she threw her hands in the air.

"What's crazy?" A woman's voice asked out of nowhere, scaring the shit out of her causing her to jump in her seat.

"You almost gave me a heart attack," Kamala yelled as she put her hand over her chest and looked over at Demetria as she walked into her office.

"I knocked three times, are you alright?" Demetria asked as she sat down in the chair Dominic had just occupied minutes before.

"Girl, I'm in shock right now!" Kamala replied as she massaged her forehead, since she felt a migraine forming.

"What happened?" Demetria asked with a frown on her face.

Sighing, "You know that Desmond and I have started seeing each other, so I decided to end things with Dominic," Kamala stated as she leaned back in her chair.

"I didn't know about you and Desmond being together, but I did know about the date you two went on. Plus, it's about damn time," Demetria stated smiling.

"I feel the same way, but now Dominic just declared his undying love and is determined to win me as if I'm some object to be fought over," Kamala replied as she shook her head again.

"So when did you tell him it was over?" Demetria asked as she leaned back in her chair.

"As a matter of fact, it just happens not even two minutes before you walked in," Kamala stated as she felt like her life was spiraling out of control.

"So he came here, and you told him it was over, but he's still determined to win you over?" Demetria asked.

"That about sums it up, and now I have to figure out how to tell Desmond about this mess," Kamala replied as she dreaded
Desmond's reaction.

"From a legal perspective, do you feel this could be a dangerous situation?" Demetria asked as she went into lawyer mode.

"No, I don't think Dominic would hurt me, I just wish he could understand that I have moved on," Kamala said while she tried to think of a way to get Dominic to think rationally.

"Well, if you need any legal help or if you need a partner in crime to beat a Negro down, I'm just a phone call away," Demetria joked causing Kamala to chuckle and shake her head as Demetria stood up.

"I'll figure this out, but I'll keep that in mind," Kamala replied while Demetria walked to the office door.

"Alright, keep me posted," Demetria said as she opened the door.

"I will Sis, and thank you," Kamala said smiling.

"You're welcome," Demetria replied before she walked out of the door and closed it behind her.

Taking a deep breath, Kamala knew that she needed to talk to Desmond about the situation, but it had to wait until later with their busy schedules, and she hoped that Desmond didn't freak out.

Chapter Eighteen

The following week, Kamala was in the boardroom getting ready for a status meeting with the Vice-Presidents when she thought about the craziness that had become her life. She had only seen Desmond a few times in passing at the office since they both had such a busy schedule that week. She was starting to miss him.

Then Dominic kept sending extravagant gifts such as jewelry, enormous amounts of flowers each day, until her office, and home started to look like a garden. It got to the point where she had started giving the flowers to coworkers. Then she had Kevin to refuse the deliveries.

Dominic then started popping up at her meetings and dinners with clients at local restaurants. She had Kevin and Nicole to increase their security duties when she wasn't home. So they had become her shadow. Kamala tried not to let his actions scare her, but it was hard not to when he kept calling and showing up unannounced. Trying to keep things civil between them, she was trying to deal with this situation on her own without getting everyone else involved, but each day became harder than the last.

"Kamala, are you alright?" Reyna asked as she down beside her at the table.

"Yeah, I'm fine, it's just a stressful week and I'm glad we're having drinks tonight at my house," Kamala replied, feeling bad for lying.

"Me too, after traveling and signing three new artist this week, I need a drink too," Reyna joked as the rest of the group walked into the room.

"Did I hear someone say drinks?" Alondra asked as she sat down on the left side of Reyna and Demetria sat on right side of Kamala with Rozlynn on the right side of Demetria.

"Yes, after this crazy week, I need a few strong drinks," Kamala replied while she shook her head as her love triangle situation replayed in her mind.

"Would this have anything to do with our earlier conversation?" Demetria asked as she narrowed her eyes at Kamala.

Sighing, "It's not just that! It's work and my personal life, and I'm just tired," Kamala confessed.

"Why don't we just have drinks tonight and relax, because this week has been crazy for me too, so I understand," Alondra suggested as they all looked at Kamala with concerned on their faces.

"I'll call Tazmin to see if she can make it, because she needs a break too," Rozlynn added.

"Well, you know I'll be there! So let's get this meeting started, because I have another meeting in thirty minutes," Demetria stated as she looked around the room.

As the meeting progressed, Kamala tried to focus on the matter at hand, but she felt like her life was out of control, and she didn't know how to fix it.

After the meeting as everyone was walking out, Kamala started collecting her things when she realized Demetria was still sitting beside her. "Are you going to tell me what's really going on with you?" Demetria asked as the last person walked out of the room.

Sighing, Kamala tossed her papers on the table, "To be honest, I don't even know where to start! My life is so fucked up," Kamala replied as tears came to her eyes.

"Start with the situation involving Dominic," Demetria suggested as she handed Kamala a tissue from the box on the table.

"This guy has lost his damn mind! He is showing up at my home, and somehow, he's showing up at my dinner meetings. Plus, he is always calling me," Kamala confessed as she gently wiped her cheeks try not to disturb her make-up.

"Kamala, you need to get a restraining order, and have Kevin and Nicole with you at all times," Demetria suggested as she covered Kamala's hand that was lying on the table with her own.

"I'm trying not to involve the courts, because it would ruin his football career. Plus, I would have to deal with the media more than I do now," Kamala replied as her tears kept coming.

"Maybe he should be thinking about his career before he started stalking you," Demetria demanding.

"You're right, but I have Kevin and Nicole with me at all times unless I'm at home, where the gate guards know to look out for Dominic," Kamala stated while she wiped away the last of her tears.

"What does Desmond have to say about this?" Demetria asked causing her tears to start all over again.

"That's my other problem, it's like he's been avoiding me all week," Kamala revealed causing Demetria to sigh.

"Have you had a chance to talk to him about the Dominic situation?" Demetria asked. "Hell, we've only said a few words to each other all week, and at night he claims to be so busy. So I don't push the issue," Kamala replied as she felt her heart breaking.

"You need to head to the studio and make time for you two to talk about this. Kamala, this is profoundly serious," Demetria stated as she picked up her papers off the table.

Running her hand through her hair, "You're right! I am heading there now before I head to my next meeting," Kamala replied as they both stood up, and she picked up her papers again.

"Good, and I'll see you tonight at your place," Demetria said as they walked out of the boardroom.

"I'll have the drinks and glasses ready," Kamala joked causing Demetria to chuckle before they went to separate ways.

Taking a deep breath, Kamala decided to drop her papers off at her office, and then she was going to start straightening out her life, beginning with Desmond.

Standing outside of the studio, Kamala took a deep breath before she pushed the door open. When she stepped into the room, she gasped at the scene before her. On the sofa was Riley laying on top of Desmond as she was kissing him. Hearing her gasp, they both looked at her. Riley had a smirk on her face while Desmond looked like a deer caught in headlights before he pushed Riley off of him.

"Kamala, please let me explain," he pleaded as tears fell down her cheek, but she quickly wiped them away.

"There isn't anything to explain, now I can see why you were so busy," she yelled in a voice full of rage, before she walked out of the room, wishing she were anywhere, but there at that moment.

Feeling him grab her arm, which she jerked out of his grasp while she faced him head on, "Kamala, it's not what you think, she kissed me," he pleaded as he tried to grab her hand, but she evaded his grasp.

"Desmond, I'm not stupid! You had to know who you were fucking kissing. I was a damn fool to believe that you could ever love me, but you know what I just realized? I'm too good of a woman to put up with this shit.

So go back to Riley and I'll move on with my life," she yelled before storming off as she felt her emotions getting the best of her.

Kamala ran inside the open doors of the elevator and quickly pressed the button to close the doors, as Desmond ran behind her calling her name.

Leaning against the elevator wall when the doors closed, with her tears pouring down her face, Kamala couldn't figure out what she did to deserve all the shit going on in her life. She realized that no one was going to treat her second best anymore.

Watching Kamala break down in the elevator as the doors closed, broke his heart. Taking a deep breath as he tried to figure out how to get Kamala back, he realized Riley was still in his studio.

Walking into the studio to find Riley sitting in front of the soundboard, "What in the hell were you thinking?" he yelled causing her to jump in her seat.

"Desmond, I know you said you needed time to yourself, but I missed you," Riley replied as she walked up to him, but he stepped back.

"If I remember correctly, I told you that we weren't meant to be together. Also that you needed to move on," he stated as he narrowed his eyes at her as he felt his anger level escalate.

Running her hand down his chest, "Desmond, you know that we were meant to be together," she whispered before she tried to kiss him, but he stepped back as his nostrils started to flare.

"I think it's time for you to leave and never come back," he suggested as he pointed to the door.

"What if I don't want to leave just yet?" she asked as she tried to approach him again.

"Then I'll make you leave!" his sister yelled causing him to look over at the door to see Kingsley standing there, and she quickly tossed her purse on the couch and looked at Riley.

"Riley, if I was you, I would leave while I could," Desmond suggested as he tried not to laugh at how scared Riley looked as she looked over at Kingsley.

Grabbing her purse, "We'll discuss this later," Riley said as she headed for the door.

"There isn't anything to discuss, we are over," Desmond replied as he looked right into her eyes so she would get the message.

"It's over! So leave my brother alone or you will deal with me," Kingsley demanded as she stepped up to Riley, who was on her way to the door.

Instead of saying anything, Riley walked out of the studio after giving Desmond one more look.

The moment the door closed, "What in the hell am I going to do to fix this shit?" Desmond yelled as he fell back onto the sofa.

"First, tell me what happened, then we can figure out how to fix it," Kingsley suggested as she moved her purse and sat down beside Desmond.

"I have just lost the woman I love, because of Riley. Not to mention that I've been so busy all week, she thinks Riley is the reason," Desmond revealed as he remembered the pain in Kamala's eyes when she looked at him.

"What did Riley do?" Kingsley asked with a frown on her face.

"Since I've been working day and night all week, I decided to lay on the couch and take a nap. So when I felt someone kissing me, I thought it was Kamala, but then I heard the door open and someone gasp. When I opened my eyes, Riley was laying on top of me and Kamala was standing there with tears in her eyes," Desmond confessed as he ran his hand over his head and sighed.

"What did Kamala say?" Kingsley asked as she shook her head.

"Just that she should never have believed that I loved her. Now she knew why I was too busy to spend time with her," he replied as he thought about the pain in her voice as she yelled at him.

"Desmond, do you really love Kamala?" Kingsley asked as she narrowed her eyes at him.

Jumping up and facing his sister as his anger flared, "Hell yes, I love her, how can you ask me that?" he demanded.

"I hate to say this, but you are going to have the fight of your life on your hands to get her back. If you really love her then pull out all the stops and don't give up," Kingsley stated as she stood up in front of him.

Blowing out a deep breath and leaning back on the edge of the soundboard stand, "Sis, I can't lose her! She means everything to me," he whispered as a tear rolled down his cheek and it felt as if someone was squeezing his heart.

"You'll figure it out, just give her time to cool off. It also wouldn't hurt to get Tazmin and her sisters on your side to help," Kingsley suggested causing him to nod his head at the idea.

"You're right! If anyone can help me, it's the Foster sisters," Desmond stated as he started to brainstorm ideas to get his woman back.

Chapter Nineteen

"Girl, I would have punched him in his damn face," Reyna yelled from her seat between Alondra and Rozlynn. While Kamala, Tazmin, and Demetria sat on the sofa across from them as they all were drinking margaritas.

"Shit, at that point I was trying not to laugh. Evan was so upset with Chicken Alfredo all over his head, and the waiter was getting fussed out by the manager," Alondra stated as the group laughed at the story of her latest date with Evan Richards, a real estate tycoon based in Chicago.

"Before the accident, was the date going alright?" Kamala asked before taking a sip of her drink, as she tried to hide that she felt as if her heart had been ripped out.

"It was alright, but I think we would be better as friends. He just gave off that Playboy vibe. Plus every five minutes while we were at the restaurant, a different woman came up to our table to say hello," Alondra replied before she finished her drink and then started to refill everyone's glasses from the pitcher on the coffee table.

"At least you can see you two at least being friends because my date with Roger Clemens was a disaster," Rozlynn added before she sighed dramatically causing the group to chuckle.

Listening to her friend's drama, helped a little to get her mind off of Desmond's betrayal and Dominic's stalking ways. Then sometimes she found herself fighting her tears as she replayed the scene in the studio from earlier that day.

Shaking her head, Kamala was determined to forget her drama for one night. "What happened?" Kamala asked before taking another sip of her drink that seemed like the perfect remedy to her hectic day.

"First, Roger was thirty minutes late, then he had the nerve to ask if I could drive us to the restaurant. Then he had the balls to ask me to pay for dinner," Rozlynn replied causing the ladies to laugh hysterically at the outraged look on her face.

Gasping for air, "Please tell me you cursed that fool out?" Tazmin joked while she and Kamala leaned on each other as they laughed.

"When he asked me to pay for dinner, I was at my boiling point and before I knew it, I had thrown my red wine in his face. Plus, since we were at Gibson's, I let Daniel know that my date was covering dinner before I walked out," Rozlynn stated as the group broke out into laughter again. Daniel Chambers was the manager of Gibson's restaurant and also a close friend of theirs.

"I think I have all of you beat for dating horror stories for this week," Demetria stated as she finished her drink.

"I have got to hear this," Tazmin joked as everyone looked over at Demetria.

"Well I had a date with Kel Lucas, so when I get to the restaurant, I see a lady sitting at a table with him. So already I'm guessing that the date was already over. So I walk up to the table, and he hugged me and introduced me to his business partner at his law firm, Leslie Graves. At that point, I'm wondering why his partner was there for our date. So as I'm about to ask, I feel her hand on my thigh," Demetria stated causing the group to hang onto her every word with their mouths wide open.

"So I jumped up and asked her what the hell was she doing, then Kel revealed that he and Leslie are lovers and wanted me to join in. Before I knew what had happened, I had punched him in his face and walked out of the restaurant," she continued. Before the group fell into fits of laughter as Demetria chugged the rest of her drink and refilled her glass.

Gasping for air, "Your date takes the cake! I've never been propositioned for a ménage before," Reyna joked shaking her head.

"I was so damn mad when I got home; I had to have a session with my punching bag before I could calm down," Demetria stated causing Kamala to chuckle.

They all knew that Demetria had a quick temper, and her punching bag helped her release her stress and not catch a criminal charge.

"Damn Kamala, I'm glad we are off the market," Tazmin joked causing Kamala to instantly stop laughing while she felt tears come to her eyes.

Sighing, "I hate to break it to you, but I'm back on the market as of today," Kamala revealed. Then she wiped the tears from her cheek and then gulped down the rest of her drink.

"Hold up, I'm confused! When we talked earlier, you and Desmond were together. So, what happened since then?" Demetria asked as she handed Kamala a tissue from the box on the coffee table.

"Hold on! I didn't even know that you two were even dating except for that one dinner," Reyna stated as Alondra nodded her head in agreement.

"Kamala, why don't you start from the beginning so that everyone can catch up," Tazmin suggested as she refilled Kamala's glass.

"Alright, the night Tazmin had the boys, Desmond took me home and invited me to his place for dinner. During dinner, we both admitted that we loved each other all these years. Then one thing led to another and we ended up in bed," Kamala confessed as her tears continue to fall as she thought about the passion and love she thought they had shared that night then she realized it was all a lie.

"It's about damn time! We all were getting ready to have an intervention with you two," Reyna joked causing Kamala to chuckle.

"So what happened after you two finally came together?" Rozlynn asked with a frown on her face.

"We spent the whole weekend together! Saturday, we had dinner with his family and Sunday, we were with Tazmin and Adonis," Kamala replied before taking a sip of her drink.

"So what happened in a matter of three weeks?" Tazmin asked as she leaned forward in her seat.

"I guess you could say our lives got in the way, with our hectic schedules. We have barely said two words to each other this week. So today after talking with Demetria about my situation with Dominic, I went to the studio to talk to Desmond about the Dominic situation, but instead I found Desmond laying on the sofa with Riley on top of him and they were making out," Kamala said as she tried to wipe away her tears, but they just kept coming as her emotions got the best of her. Tazmin pulled her into her arms and hugged her.

"I can't believe Desmond would do something like that," Demetria stated as she handed Kamala some more issue.

"Me neither! We all could see how you felt about each other. So why would he fuck it all up now?" Tazmin asked as her voice became hard and emotionless.

Pulling away from Tazmin and wiping her cheek, "I don't know, but now I just can't deal with anymore drama. Then to make matters worse, Dominic is calling me so much I may have to change my number," Kamala added as she released a shaky breath.

"What's going on with Dominic? That's the Ex you ran into at Club Heat, right?" Reyna asked before taking a sip of her drink.

"Yes, that's him! We had gone out to dinner a few times before everything happened with Desmond. So I knew that I needed to let Dominic know that I was seeing someone and that we could still be friends," Kamala stated before wiping her cheek again.

"Let me guess, he didn't take the news that well?" Alondra asked before finishing her drink.

"That's an understatement! He declared that he wasn't going to lose me again, and that he'll prove he is the better man," Kamala confessed causing the ladies to sigh and shake their heads.

"So what's happened since you two talked?" Rozlynn asked.

"He has been calling me nonstop, sending me jewelry, flowers, and candy, and he has even been popping up everywhere I go," Kamala stated before she finished her drink and sat her glass down on the table.

"This is getting scary and dangerous, and you need to up your security and get a restraining order," Rozlynn suggested.

"After everything started happening, I take Kevin and Nicole with me everywhere unless I'm at home, where the guard at the gate knows the situation. Shit, I even have Kevin and Nicole going through my deliveries as a precaution," Kamala replied as she suddenly felt drained.

"Kamala, this is a lot to deal with! So, just know that we're here for you," Tazmin stated as she hugged Kamala, which triggered more tears.

Pulling back, "I'll be fine, and I have plenty of work to keep me busy. Plus I have Kevin and Nicole to watch my back," Kamala said as she wiped her cheek and Demetria refilled her glass.

"Just know that we got your back, and we all can pay Mr. Dominic a visit," Demetria joked causing the group to chuckle.

As they continued to gossip, Kamala hoped that her life would return to normal because she didn't know how much more drama she could take.

Sitting in his game room with Adonis, Spencer, Liam, Gunner, Rico, Ryder, and Adam, they were watching the last five seconds of a Bulls' basketball game. Desmond tried to figure out how his life turned upside down in a matter of five minutes.

"Bro, what going on with you?" Ryder asked causing everyone's attention to go to Desmond.

"I was going to ask the same thing," Adonis added as he frowned at Desmond.

"I thought you would be on cloud nine since you and Kamala got together," Adam joked.

"After today, Kamala will never speak to me again," Desmond stated causing the group of guys to groan.

"Man, what did you do?" Spencer asked before he finished his beer.

"To be honest, I'm still confused about what happened! One minute I'm taking a nap on the sofa in the studio, when someone started kissing me. So I thought it was Kamala. Then the next thing I know, I hear someone gasp and when I opened my eyes, I see Kamala standing at the door with tears in her eyes and Riley on top of me," Desmond confessed as his stomach felt like it was in knots as he realized how bad he had hurt Kamala.

"Damn!" Adam stated as he shook his head.

"Did you try to explain to Kamala what happened?" Liam asked with a frown on his face.

"Yes, I did, but she wasn't hearing it! Plus, she thinks Riley is the reason I've been so busy lately," Desmond replied before running his hand over his face.

"You have got to fix this quick with Kamala, because when my wife and the girls hear about this tonight at ladies night, it's going to be rough," Adonis suggested causing Desmond to groan.

"He's right! You know how protective they are over each other, not to mention that all this happened at the studio," Gunner added.

"Let's not forget our crazy sister when she finds out," Ryder added.

Sighing, "Kingsley already knows since she came to the studio right after it happened," Desmond stated as he replayed the whole event in his mind.

"And you're still breathing! What did she say?" Adam joked causing the group to chuckle.

"To make a long story short, after Kamala left, I went back to the studio and told Riley that we were over and that she needed to leave me alone, but she acted like she wasn't hearing that. Which is when Kingsley walked in and then she threated Riley to leave me alone. After Riley ran out, me and Kingsley talked and she suggested that I give Kamala some time to calm down, and while I was waiting that I needed to get the girls on my side," Desmond replied before drinking some of his beer.

"Your sister is right! Kamala needs some time, and as for my wife and sisters-in-law, I'll help you talk with them if you want," Adonis suggested just as the doorbell rang.

"That must be the pizza, I'll get it," Ryder said as he jumped up from his recliner next to Desmond.

"Man, all I can say is, when you talk to Tazmin and the girls, just be honest. Plus, you all have been friends for years," Spencer suggested.

"You're right, I just don't know where to start cleaning up this mess," Desmond said as he finished his beer.

"You can start by telling us what the hell you were thinking hurting Kamala like that?" Tazmin yelled causing Desmond to spit out the beer in his mouth before he looked up to see Tazmin and her sisters standing in the doorway looking pissed.

"Tazmin, let me explain," Desmond pleaded, but when Tazmin's eyes narrowed in on him, he looked at Adonis and the guys for help, but they were just as shocked as he was.

Clearing his throat seem to get Adonis's attention, "Baby!" Adonis started as he walked up to Tazmin, "Why don't we all sit down and talk about this," he continued as he led his wife and sister-in-laws over to the recliner across from the guys, but her eyes never left Desmond which caused him gulp.

"Now ladies, as Desmond tries to explain, please keep an open mind," Spencer suggested, but all he received was an eye roll from the ladies.

"It better be a damn good explanation as to why our sister is at home heartbroken and in tears," Demetria demanded causing his heart to ache at the thought of Kamala hurt and crying because of him.

Taking a deep breath, before he started, Desmond felt like a defendant in court and those five women were his jury. So he knew that he had to plead his case and throw himself at the mercy of the court if he wanted them to help him win Kamala back.

Chapter Twenty

Gasping as he pounded into her throbbing womanhood, Kamala loved the wild passion that seemed to flow through their bodies as they performed their dance of desire. Taking each other to the next level as a light sheen of sweat covered their hot bodies. Running her shaky hand down Desmond's back, she could feel the way his muscles constricted with each thrust, turning her on even more.

Moaning and thrashing her head back and forth, Kamala started to meet each of his powerful thrust with one of her own. The friction of their pelvises grinding against each other sent shockwaves straight to her core causing her to scream out again. Gasping for air as she felt every nerve ending in her body go on high alert, Kamala pulled his magical lips down to hers, just as she screamed out in ecstasy and stars flashed before her eyes.

Jumping up in her bed panting and sweating from head to toe, "Not this shit again!" Kamala yelled as she sat on the edge of her bed. Shaking her head as the dream seemed to play over and over again in her head as her body felt as if it was on fire. Her womanhood throbbed with need; Kamala squeezed her legs together hoping for some relief. She began to wonder what she had done for her life to be so fucked up. Sure, she went to a few dinners with Dominic, but that didn't give him the right to start stalking her. Sure, she finally told Desmond how she felt about him and thought they loved each other when she found him making out with his so-called ex.

Sighing and wiping the tears from her cheek, Kamala realized maybe it was time to look for happiness within herself, instead of expecting it from a man. Then with that revelation, Kamala pulled her shoulders back, dried her cheeks, and decided that day was about Tazmin and her family as they visited their parents' graves. Standing up and walking over to her closet, Kamala knew it was going to be a stressful day for them all, and she was determined to be there for her sisters when they needed her.

Looking at her clothes, Kamala decided to wear her black stretch jersey dress that hugged her curves perfectly but was still appropriate for the occasion, along with her gold metallic heels and gold accessories.

Heading to the shower, Kamala hoped that her friends made it through the day as they grieved for their parents.

Just as she was leaving home with Kevin and Nicole, her doorbell rang causing them all to frown because she wasn't expecting anyone. When Kevin answer the door, she was shocked to see Dominic standing there with a bouquet of flowers in his hand.

Walking closer to the door as Kevin blocked his way of walking into her home, "Dominic, what are you doing here?" she asked as Nicole moved to her side with her hand on her gun.

"I hadn't heard from you, so I came by to make sure you alright," he replied as he once again tried to enter her home, but Kevin blocked his way again.

"Dominic, I'm heading out for the day and I'll call you later so we can talk," Kamala stated. Then she saw that look in his eyes again causing a chill to go down her spine.

"That's cool, I just wanted to check on you. Enjoy your day and I look forward to that call so we can talk about us," Dominic replied as he handed her the roses that she took with shaking hands.

"Dominic, we already had this talk, but I'll still call you later," Kamala replied before Kevin ushered him back to his car.

"It's something about him that I don't trust," Nicole stated as she and Kamala stood in the front door as Kevin made sure Dominic got in his car and left.

"Me too, but right now I need to get over to Tazmin's," Kamala replied as she grabbed her purse off the foyer table. Then she and Nicole walked outside heading to the car where Kevin was waiting.

As she climbed into the back of the car, Kamala started to wonder how Dominic was able to get past the guards at the gate. She was also going to make sure that the management got an earful from her when she returned home.

Arriving at Tazmin's, Kamala took a deep breath before ringing the doorbell. The day had already started off crazy, and she knew she had to hold it together. When the door opened, a smile instantly came to her face when she saw Spencer. "Hello Spencer," she greeted as she walked into the house and he hugged her.

"Right back at you," he replied as they pulled apart and he closed the door.

"How have you been doing?" she asked as they walked into the living room where everyone had gathered.

"I can't complain, how about you?" he replied smiling as they walked over to where Tazmin and her sisters were sitting.

"I can't either," she replied smiling.

"I was starting to wonder where you were," Tazmin greeted as she stood up looking stunning as ever in her black lace dress as she hugged Kamala.

"Let's just say I had an unexpected visitor, so that's why I'm late," Kamala replied causing Tazmin and her sisters to frown as they stood up too.

"Who was it?" Demetria asked as she hugged Kamala next followed by Alondra, Reyna, and Rozlynn.

"Let's not get into my drama today, I'm here to support you guys," Kamala replied as they all narrowed their eyes at Kamala just as the doorbell rang again.

"Just because we need to head to the grave site now doesn't mean we are not going to talk about this later," Tazmin warned causing Kamala to smile.

"Yes ma'am!" Kamala joked as she saluted Tazmin causing the group the chuckle as they shook their heads.

"It seems our last guest has arrived," Alondra stated causing the group to look toward the door to see Desmond walking into the room, looking handsome as ever in a black suit with a black dress shirt and a navy silk tie. Looking behind him, she saw his family had accompanied him.

"Lord, is this a test?" Kamala whispered causing the ladies to chuckle as a blush rose to her cheeks.

When he looked into her eyes, Kamala knew that her day had just gotten more complicated, causing her to sigh as she looked the other way.

Standing at the grave site of Evan and Patricia Foster, Kamala stood between Tazmin and Demetria holding their hands as Pastor Roy said a prayer. Kamala could tell that her sisters were trying to stay strong as silent tears fell from behind their dark sunglasses. Their strength was one of the things Kamala admired about those ladies; she had come to call her sisters.

When the pastor finished, and their guests had paid their respects, it was finally time for the sisters to pay their respects. Being the eldest, Tazmin was the first to go. So with Kamala on one side and Adonis on her other, they approached the grave.

Wiping her cheek, "Hey mom and dad, it's another year later and so much has happened," Tazmin started as her tears flowed freely down her face. "I finally slowed down like you had suggested so long ago and I met my soulmate. We are married now, and we just had your first grandchildren," she continued as she cried and leaned on

Adonis while Kamala rubbed her back and handed her some tissues.

"My husband's name is Adonis, and I know you would have loved him as much as I do," Tazmin stated causing Adonis to smile before he kissed her. "Your grandsons' names are Hunter and Hayden; I will make sure they know about you. They remind me a lot of how Reyna and Rozlynn were at that age," Tazmin joked causing the group to chuckle.

"They are total opposites and are very stubborn just like their aunts. I hope I can be as good of parents to them as you were to us. You gave us the tools we needed to be independent and strong," Tazmin cried as her emotions started to get the best of her causing Adonis and Kamala to hold onto her tighter.

"You would be so proud of the girls. They have grown to be strong, smart, and beautiful women and I hope I did right by them after you were gone, because I love them with all I have and I love you too," Tazmin finished just as her sisters walked over and hugged her and Kamala as they all cried together.

"Hi mom and dad, we are making you proud by continuing your legacy. We miss you so much, and there isn't a day that goes by that we don't think about you," Demetria started as Adonis stepped back and she took his spot.

On the other side of Kamala was Alondra, who was sobbing causing Tazmin and Demetria to help hold her up until Liam came forward and led her back to the car.

Then Kamala stood between Reyna and Rozlynn with Tazmin and Demetria at their other sides, "Hi mom and dad, when you were taken from us, we were just entering that awkward teenage phase, but because of Tazmin, and the values you taught us, we are finally happy and not having nightmares anymore. You would be so proud of the way she continues to check on us and love us as a mother would. Demetria and Alondra are following in your career path to keep your legacy alive," Reyna started before her emotions got the best of her and Demetria led her back to the car.

"With Alondra and Demetria following in your footsteps, we wanted to follow in our big sister's footsteps, so her legacy will continue. We all miss you so much, and it's so hard to go through the day without you, but we have each other, and your adopted daughter Kamala. We help each other the way you raised us to do. I know you are watching over us and we all will continue to make you proud. Love you," Rozlynn finished, wiping her cheek, just as she was overwhelmed with emotion. Gunner walked her back to the car leaving Tazmin and Kamala standing there holding each other.

"Hey mom and dad, we may not have known each other long, but you still welcomed me into your home and hearts and for that I could never repay you. Each day that goes by, we feel your presence and know that we have our guardian angels watching over us. I can still remember the last dinner we all had together, and you telling us not to go boy crazy and keep our heads in our books during college," Kamala said causing Tazmin and the group the chuckle.

"Then I remember you pulling me aside and telling me that I was your daughter and no matter what I could always count on you. You also said that it was me and Tazmin's job to keep the rest of our sisters in line. That night Tazmin and I made you a promise to keep our family together, and now our family has gotten bigger. So rest in peace, knowing we will keep that promise. I will always love you," Kamala finished as her emotions overcame her and Tazmin as they held each other until someone pulled her into their arms.

When she looked up, she saw that it was Desmond. Instead of pushing him away as her mind was telling her to, she held onto him as he led her to the family car. On the ride back to Tazmin's house, she welcomed the comfort his arms provided, but she couldn't let herself get too comfortable there.

"You had dad wrapped around your finger," Reyna yelled as they all sat around the dining room table reminiscing.

"Like you can talk! Who had to have dad tuck her into bed until she was twelve?" Alondra joked causing the group to laugh.

"If we are being honest, Demetria had you all beat!" Tazmin added causing Demetria to roll her eyes.

"Yeah right! You had mom and dad wrapped around your finger too. Tazmin could do no wrong in their eyes," Demetria replied.

"She does have a point," Alondra added.

"Then Kamala joined the family, and they had two favorites," Rozlynn stated.

"You are so wrong! I still remember when Tazmin and I went to our first college party and got drunk. Then this nut called your dad laughing and screaming before she asked him to come and get us. The next morning, we both had bad hangovers and he made us sit in the kitchen as he gave us a long lecture, and then he turned on the blender to make his morning smoothie with a smirk on his face," Kamala stated causing the group to laugh.

"That was the last party we went to during college that we got drunk," Tazmin added smiling.

"We had some good times back then, without a care in the world," Alondra stated with a faraway look in her eyes.

"Yes, we did, and there are many more to be had," Kamala added as she covered Alondra's hand on the table and smiled at her.

"You are so right! So let's toast to mom and dad and here's to continuing their legacy of living life to the fullest," Rozlynn said as she raised her glass with everyone following her lead.

"Mom and dad!" everyone cheered before clicking their glasses together.

Looking down at her watch, "Guys, I hate to leave, but I have a busy day tomorrow," Kamala stated as she stood up and started to hug everyone.

"I understand, and we will talk about that situation later," Tazmin whispered when they hugged.

"Alright," Kamala replied as she gathered her purse.

After hugging the ladies, Kamala hugged Adonis, his family, and then Desmond's family.

When she came to him, she just looked up at him, "Thank you for helping me earlier," she stated as she tried to control the anxiety she was feeling.

"Anytime, I'm always here," he replied, but she just nodded her head before walking to the front door with Tazmin at her side.

"Do you need one of us to go with you home?" Tazmin asked once they were alone.

Shaking her head, "No, I have Kevin and Nicole downstairs waiting for me, and once I get home, they will check the doors and windows before they leave. Plus, the guards at the gate are there too," Kamala replied.

"Alright, call me if you need anything," Tazmin stated as they hugged.

Pulling apart, "I will! Love you and I will talk to you later," Kamala replied as she opened the door and walked out.

"Love you too, sister," Tazmin said before Kamala walked toward the elevator.

"Kamala!" A male voice called just before she could press the down button.

Turning around, she found Desmond walking toward her, causing her breath to hitch and her heart rate to race faster, the closer he came toward her until he was in front of her.

"What do you want Desmond?" she asked as her hands started to shake slightly.

"I want a chance to explain what really happened between me and Riley, because it wasn't what you thought," he replied causing her to suddenly feel drained.

"Desmond, there is no need to explain. You are a grown man and if Riley is your choice, then so be it," Kamala stated as she pushed the down button.

"I don't want Riley, I want and love you," he confessed before he closed the distance between them and kissed her, causing her to moan as she felt the softness of his lips and sampled his minty taste.

All too soon the sexual haze in her head cleared, and she pulled away from him. Watching him as she stepped into the open elevator, "Desmond, you hurt me and betrayed my trust. I don't see how I can get past that," she stated as tears flooded her eyes. Then as the doors started to slowly close, she watched him with his pleading eyes. Kamala had to resist the urge to run into his arms.

Once the doors closed, Kamala leaned back against the wall as her tears fell while she remembered his touch, his kisses, and his taste. Then she remembered the pain she felt when she walked into the studio that day, and Kamala realized she didn't know if her heart would ever be the same.

Chapter Twenty-One

After taking a long shower and pulling on her red maxi dress, Kamala walked downstairs to see Kevin and Nicole waiting for her as they sat on the sofa in the living room.

"We checked the entire house, and everything is locked," Kevin said as they followed her to the foyer.

"Kamala, are you sure you don't want us to stick around?" Nicole asked causing Kamala to smile.

"Guys, you have this house secured like Fort Knox. Plus, I'm headed to bed anyway," Kamala replied as she led them to the front door.

"Make sure you call us if you need anything," Kevin stated before he opened the door.

"I will, plus I have you on speed dial as number three," she replied as they both nodded their heads and walked out of the door and closed it behind them, which she also locked.

Taking a deep breath, Kamala walked back into a living room and over to the bar, where she poured herself a glass of white wine just as her doorbell rang.

With a smile on her face as she rushed to unlock the door, "What did you forget?" she asked as she opened it, only to freeze in shock when she saw Dominic standing there with a smile on his face.

Fear almost paralyzed her, "Dominic, what are you doing here?" she asked as she felt her hands start to shake.

"I know you said that you would call, but I was in the area, so I stopped by," he replied to causing Kamala to get even more nervous since her home was out in the middle of nowhere, so she knew he was lying.

"I'm sorry you came all the way here, but I have a busy day tomorrow, so I'm headed to bed," Kamala stated as she realized she shouldn't have had Kevin and Nicole leave so soon.

"Can we just sit down and talk for a few minutes, and then I will leave and never bother you again?" Dominic asked, but deep-down Kamala knew that she couldn't trust him with her there alone.

"Can we get together for lunch tomorrow, because today has tired me out and I need some sleep," she replied as she saw anger flash in his eyes, sending a chill down her spine.

"I really wish you hadn't done this," he stated in a hard tone as he stepped forward, but Kamala quickly tried to shut the door.

Releasing a scream as she tried to push the door closed, Kamala put all her strength behind the door, but all too soon he pushed it open.

"Dominic, just get out of my house!" she screamed as he backed her into the living room. Then she looked for anything she could use to defend herself as her heart began beating out of her chest.

"All I wanted to do was love you, but that wasn't good enough for you," he yelled as he rushed her and pulled her into his arms as tears blinded her vision.

Trying to fight him by clawing out his eyes, Kamala tried to think of a way to call for help.

"You don't love me, so get the fuck off me," she yelled at she continued to struggle. Looking into his eyes, she didn't see the man she once loved. He looked possessed, and she was determined not to go down without a fight as she tried to knee him in his private area while continuing to claw out his eyes.

"Be still, Bitch!" he yelled., before smacking her on the left side of her face with such force, it knocked her down onto the floor between the coffee table and sofa.

Kamala gasped for air. "Dominic, get the hell out of my house!" she yelled as she tried to get up. Suddenly he was beside her, kicking her in her stomach. She could barely pull in breath the pain was so intense as she curled into a ball to protect herself best, she could from his attacks.

"Shut the fuck up! I'm in control here, and you will do what the fuck I say," he yelled as he kicked her again causing her to scream.

"Please stop!" she groaned through her tears as he climbed on top of her and forced her onto her back.

Grabbing her by her hair, he spoke rabidly, spit flying from his mouth. "Don't you understand how much I love you, and you would rather be a hoe and fuck that producer dude at the Label?" he yelled as he smacked her again causing her to taste the rusty taste of blood as it filled her mouth.

"What are you talking about?" she whispered as she looked at him through her tears, only to see nothing but rage in his eyes, filling her with more fear.

"Bitch, I've been following you. So don't try to play games with me," Dominic yelled before he punched her in her left eye causing her to gasp.

She became dizzy, as he kept punching her until she lost count. It was as if her body was shutting down, as the pain seemed to become unbearable.

"Say that you are mine, Bitch!" he yelled with spit flying from his mouth as he straddled her hips.

"Yes, I'm yours!" she gasped as intense pain radiated from her head to her feet, while she endeavored to breathe.

He released the grip of her hair, violently causing her skull to bounce off the hardwood floor. She could see stars develop before her eyes. "Now I'm really going to make you mine," he yelled.

Kamala gasped as he started pulling her dress up, and she realized what he intended to do. Not giving up without a fight, she started swinging at his face, hitting him in the jaw, which caused him to fall backward.

Seeing her chance, she started kicking him as she kept swinging at him and connecting with his face and chest, as her knee connected with his manhood causing him to groan. With him momentarily stunned, Kamala made a run for the door, but he grabbed her ankle, pulling her down to the floor again.

The impact was so hard, the breath was knocked out of her. But she wasn't going to give up, as she tried kicking him in the face as he dragged her back to him.

It didn't seem to faze him as he climbed on top of her, "You are going to pay for that!" Dominic yelled as he started punching her in the face with one hand with his other hand wrapped around her throat.

As the punches kept coming, Kamala tried to shake her head as she clawed at his hand that was on her neck and his face.

"Why can't you act right? I never would have done this if you had went with the plan," he yelled as he still held her neck, but started to rip her dress baring her breasts.

Breathing hard and nauseated from pain, "Dominic, please stop!" Kamala yelled as her tears blinded her vision and the pain was radiating through her body.

"In a minute, you'll be begging me to keep going," he whispered as he laid on top of her and pinned her arms above her head.

"Never, you sick bastard!" Kamala yelled before she spit blood in his face, earning her a slap across her face.

"We'll see!" he yelled as he finished ripping her dress open to reveal that she was wearing nothing but a black thong. "What do we have here?" he continued as he pinched her nipple hard, causing Kamala to scream.

"Please stop!" she screamed as she used all her strength to reach onto the coffee table and snatching up the brass vase, she hit him on the side of his head.

Screaming with each swing, Kamala noticed he was falling off her, so she climbed from under him and ran to her desk, where she grabbed the sharp silver letter opener.

"Get the fuck out of my house before I kill you!" Kamala screamed as she slowly limped toward him causing him to look at her hand.

He looked like he was debating if he could take her, until she jabbed the letter opener at him, "I said get the fuck out!"

she yelled as she put her other hand on her stomach as the gesture could be a balm to the blinding pain.

With one last look, he quickly ran out of the door leaving it wide open. Kamala quickly limped over to it, shut it and locked it. Before sliding down the door to the floor. She could feel her body wanting to succumb to darkness that lay just beyond, but she had to get to the phone to call for help.

Trying to stand, Kamala fell back on the floor, and gasped as the pain almost paralyzed her. Through her tears, she slid half crawled across the floor over to the coffee table, where her cordless phone was lying. Kamala collapsed on the floor in tears as it hurt to breathe.

"Lord help me!" she whispered before she took the last of her energy and reached for the phone causing it to fall on the floor by her head. Sighing, she felt as if she was falling into a black hole, as she hit the call button and pressed the number two button. Taking a shallow breath just before the darkness overcame her, she heard someone answer. "Please help me!" she whispered before everything became black.

Chapter Twenty-Two

"Desmond, you two will figure this mess out, and I'll help in any way that I can," Tazmin offered as they stood in her living room.

"I hope so, she means everything to me," Desmond replied as he remembered the sadness in her eyes as the elevator doors closed earlier that day.

"Kamala just needs some time," Tazmin added as she hugged him.

He pulled back. "You're right!" he replied just as his cell phone rang. When he pulled it out, a smile came to his face as he answered it, "Hello," he greeted but all he heard was shallow breathing causing him to panic.

"Kamala!" he yelled gaining everyone's attention as his grip tightened on the phone.

"Please help me!" she whispered causing a tear to come to his eyes as he ran to the door.

"I'm coming Baby!" he yelled as he pulled the door open, but a hand grabbed his arm stopping him.

"Desmond, what's going on?" Tazmin asked as everyone stood behind her.

"Kamala sounds hurt, and I need to get to her house," he demanded.

"I'm going with you," she replied as she grabbed her purse and followed him.

"What did she say?" Adonis asked as the whole group walked onto the elevator.

"She just said please help me, then all I could hear was her shallow breathing," he replied.

"Please let my sister be alright," Tazmin cried as she pulled out her phone.

"Who are you calling?" Demetria asked. "Kevin and Nicole, they could get there before we could," Tazmin replied.

Running out of the elevator when it opened, Desmond, Tazmin, Adonis, and Desmond's family jumped into his SUV, while Tazmin's sisters and Adonis's brothers and cousin jumped into Demetria's Ford Expedition. Headed to Kamala's house, Desmond prayed that she was alright.

When they arrived at Kamala's house, they saw that Kevin and Nicole had also just pulled up.

"What's going on? We just left here an hour ago," Kevin asked as they walked up to the front door.

"We don't know; Kamala called saying, please help me," Desmond replied as Kevin tried to open the door and found it locked.

Nicole quickly unlocked the door with her key while she and Kevin drew their guns, "Stay here!" they both warned as Kevin slowly pushed open the door and they entered.

They looked around, quickly taking in the result of an attack. "Call 911," Nicole yelled as they ran into the living room, and Desmond followed.

When he looked on the floor, his knees almost gave out. There on the floor was Kamala with blood and bruises covering her body with her dress ripped open, and she was unconscious. As Kevin and Nicole worked on her doing CPR, Desmond kneeled down beside Kevin as he held her delicate hand as tears flooded his eyes.

"What the hell!" Tazmin yelled as she and her sisters took in her state and became hysterical, with Adonis and his brothers trying to soothe them.

"Did anyone call 911?" Desmond demanded as he pulled out his phone placing the call himself, as Kevin and Nicole continued to try and save the woman he loved.

Watching Kevin press down on her chest as Nicole breathed air into her lungs, Desmond felt as if he was dying inside. Seeing her tattered body, he couldn't imagine the trauma she had gone through.

"She's breathing, but it's very shallow," Nicole yelled causing everyone to get quiet before they heard the welcomed sound of sirens.

"Who would do this to her? Kamala was the nicest person I know," Kingsley whispered.

"We know who in the hell could have done it," Tazmin yelled in a hard voice filled with rage.

"We do too!" Kevin added as the medics rushed in and pushed them out of the way as they asked Kevin and Nicole numerous questions.

"After we get her to the hospital, I want to know everything you all know," Desmond demanded. Then he watched as the medics gently lifted Kamala to the gurney and put an oxygen mask on her face and covered her body with a sheet.

"First, I'm going to call my contacts at the police department and get that bastard locked up," Kevin stated as his nostrils started to flare, and his eyes narrowed as he looked down at Kamala with her face so swollen, he almost didn't recognize her.

"You do that, while we follow them to the hospital," Desmond stated as they followed the medics out the door just as the police arrived.

"You guys go ahead, we will handle the police," Nicole stated as they put Kamala's still body in the back of the ambulance.

"Thank you so much, guys," Tazmin stated as she hugged Kevin and Nicole.

"You don't have to thank us, Kamala is our little sister and that bastard is going to pay," Nicole stated before they nodded their heads and walked over to the officers.

Jumping into his SUV again, Desmond couldn't stop his tears from falling as he replayed the scene of Kamala on the floor amidst overturned furniture in his mind. She looked so broken and helpless.

"I can't lose my sister," Tazmin whispered from the passenger seat as she looked out the window with tears pouring down her face too.

He grabbed her hand, "We are not going to lose her, she's too strong and stubborn to give up just like her big sister," Desmond replied though his chest felt as if an elephant was sitting on it.

"Desmond, you need to know everything that's been going on," Tazmin stated causing Desmond to look at her.

"Let's get to the hospital, and then we can all sit down and get everything out in the open. Right now, I need to make sure she's taking care of," Desmond replied as they pulled up to the hospital. As they jumped out of the SUV, Desmond prayed that he got another chance to tell Kamala that he loved her again.

Sitting in the waiting room going out of his mind, Desmond tried to stay calm but with each minute that went by without hearing how Kamala was doing, he became more worried.

Then Kevin and Nicole walked in, "How is she doing?" Nicole asked.

"We don't know anything yet," Desmond replied. "Did the police find the person who hurt her?" he asked as he stood in front of them.

"Hell yes, we found his ass," Kevin stated causing everyone to sigh out of relief.

"Dominic was at home with scratches all over his face and arms along with a big gash on the side of his head," Nicole added.

"Why did he do this?" Adonis asked as he stepped beside Desmond.

"We can answer that," Tazmin and Demetria said at the same time, causing everyone to look at them.

"What do you know?" Desmond asked, but he already knew that the ladies shared everything with each other.

"Do you remember when we all went a Club Heat a few weeks ago?" Demetria asked causing Desmond to nod his head.

"Yeah, that's where she ran into her ex-boyfriend right?" Desmond asked.

"Right, well they went on a few dinner dates, before you two got together. That's when she told him that she was seeing someone else, and he became determine not to lose her again," Tazmin added as she sat down in the chair behind her and put her head in her hands.

"Tazmin, are you alright?" Adonis asked as he sat down beside her as she cried.

"Hell no I'm not alright! My sister is in there fighting for her life and that bastard is still breathing," she yelled at her emotions got the best of her. "I should have protected her, I should have done something when she came to me," she yelled as Desmond sat on the other side of her as tears flowed from his eyes.

"Tazmin, you are only one person, and you are always there for us so don't you dare blame yourself for what that son of a bitch did," Demetria insisted as she handed Tazmin some tissues. "Plus, she came to me the day things started to get worse, so I could also blame myself," Demetria added.

"We could blame ourselves too, because we had a feeling that we should have stayed with her. After he showed up at her house this afternoon, before she headed to your house, but after getting on the grounds security for letting him in, and then double checking all the locks and windows Kamala insisted that we leave," Kevin stated before running his hand through his hair.

"Kevin, you and Nicole have always been there for Kamala, and I know you would have been there if she hadn't been so stubborn as usual," Tazmin stated as she dried her cheeks.

"I don't understand why she never told me all this was going on," Desmond stated as he looked around at the group.

"Desmond, I hate to tell you this, but she went to tell you after he really started stalking her and Kevin and Nicole had to increase their security duties. As a matter of fact, I was the one that convinced her that you had a right to know,"

Demetria replied she sat down beside him, and he frowned her.

"Kamala never told me about this, because if she had I never would have left her side," he said as he looked around the group.

"The day everything happened at the studio with Riley was when she was coming to tell you," Reyna stated causing his heart to feel as if it had fallen to his feet.

"Damn, I really fucked up," he cried as he put his elbows on his thighs and let his head fall as his tears fell freely.

"You couldn't have done any more than we could have, so don't you blame yourself either," Tazmin stated as she rubbed his back.

"Right now we need to focus on being there for Kamala and helping her through this," Kingsley added as she handed him some tissue.

"You're right! Kamala is all that matters right now," Desmond replied as he dried his face and prayed, she made it through this craziness in one piece so they could make things right between them.

Chapter Twenty-Three

Hours later, as they continued to wait for the word on Kamala, everyone else had headed to the cafeteria to grab some coffee, except for Tazmin and Desmond who sat together holding hands.

"Tazmin, I can't lose her," Desmond whispered as a single tear rolled down his cheek.

"I can't either, and we won't, because she's too stubborn to give up remember?" Tazmin replied just as a short and bald doctor dressed in green scrubs came into the room.

"Are you Ms. Hardwood's family?" he asked as he approached them.

They both stood up, "Yes, we are! How is my sister doing?" Tazmin asked as she tightened her hold on Desmond's hand.

"I'm Doctor Jacob and Kamala is an incredibly lucky woman! We had to rush her into surgery after we found out she was bleeding internally. We were able to fix the injuries," he replied as he looked at Tazmin and Desmond.

"What injuries did she have?" Desmond asked as his heart rate started to accelerate.

"On top of her internal injuries, she has three cracked ribs, a severe concussion from blows to the front and back of her head, her face is swollen and bruised, there's bruises around her neck were it looked like she was being choked, her chest and stomach are also bruised, and the only good thing out of this situation is that her attacker didn't rape her, since the rape kit came back negative," he replied causing them to sigh out of relief.

"Can we see her?" Tazmin asked as she wiped her cheek.

"Yes, you can if you will follow me and I'll take you to her room," Doctor Jacob replied before he led them out of the waiting room.

Still holding hands, Desmond took a deep breath to calm his racing heart since he knew that she was alright.

When they arrived outside of the hospital room door, "When you go in, you have to remember her face and body are severely swollen and bruised, and she is sleeping off the anesthesia from surgery," Doctor Jacob revealed as he looked at each of them.

"Thank you so much for saving my sister," Tazmin stated as she shook his hand.

"Yes, thank you so much," Desmond added as he also shook the doctor's hand before the doctor nodded, and then walked away.

Looking over Tazmin, and squeezing her hand, Desmond pushed open the door. The moment he looked at Kamala, he felt tears come to his eyes as he walked over to the bed.

He heard Tazmin sniffle and figured that she was crying as he continued to look at the woman who had captured his heart. Even with her face swollen and bruised, she was still the most beautiful woman that he had ever known.

"Tazmin, he has to pay for this," Desmond whispered as he felt his anger radiator from his body.

"You don't even have to worry, because when our lawyers get done with his ass, he's going to wish he was never born," Tazmin replied with rage filling her voice and her nose flaring.

"Right now, we need to band together and be there for her. It's going to take some time for her to cope with this drama," she continued as she sat down on the edge of the bed and gently held Kamala's hand.

"You're right! She's all that matters, and I plan to spend the rest of my life helping her forget this day ever happened," he stated as he gently moved Kamala's soft hair out of her face.

"Sounds like wedding bells in the near future," Tazmin joked causing a smile to touch his lips.

"If she'll have me," he replied as he peered down into her face as if to commit her facial features beneath the bruises to his memory-the features that tethered his heart long ago.

"Desmond, Kamala has loved you since the first day of freshman orientation in college, and that hasn't changed," she stated as she looked up at him.

"After the mess with Riley, I'm not so sure," he replied as he pulled a chair closer to the bed and sat down.

"Yes, she was hurt by what happened, but once you two sit down and discuss the situation, you will see that her love for you hasn't changed. I will say this though, if you hurt her again, she'll be the least of your worries," Tazmin warned as her eyes narrowed at him.

Lifting his hands up in surrender, "I understand, and I'll be the last person to hurt her," Desmond replied as he wondered how he became so lucky to have such a loyal friend as Tazmin in his life.

She stood and gently lay her hand on his shoulder. "I'm going to give you some privacy and go let the rest of the family know what's going on," Tazmin said as she slid her arm around him before she kissed Kamala's forehead.

"Thank you," Desmond replied.

"That's what family is for," she said before walking out the door.

Gently he laced his fingers with Kamala's and leaned close to her ear. "Baby, I know you have been through a lot lately, but I need you to open those beautiful brown eyes for me. Kamala, you mean so much to me, and I just can't see my life without you in it. I love you with all my heart! I want to spend every waking moment showing you just how much," he wiped the tears from his cheek and then looked out the window to calm himself.

"I love you too," he heard someone whisper. He looked up at Kamala, but she was still asleep making him think he was hearing things as he moved closer to the bed.   Then she squeezed his hand, causing him to gasp.

"Kamala baby, open your gorgeous eyes for me," he pleaded as he now stood over her, just before her eyelids began to flutter causing him to hold his breath until they finally opened.

"Hey baby," he whispered before he softly kissed her lips and pulled back.

"Hey, what happened?" she whispered in a dry raspy voice causing him to pour her a cup of water and lift it up to her lips with a straw.

"We'll get to that later, right now I just want you to get some rest," he replied as he sat the cup down on the table next to her bed and gently grabbed her hand again.

"Desmond, I'm so sorry for pushing you away," she whispered as tears came to her eyes causing his heart to ache.

"Kamala, you don't have anything to apologize for because if the situation was switched, I might have done the same thing. Let's just agree to start fresh and love each other until we are old and gray," he joked as he caressed her hand and smiled.

"And feeding each other creamed corn," she joked trying to giggle before wincing.

"Very funny! I'm going to call your nurse and let them know that you are awake. I also want you to know that I love you," he whispered as he pressed the call button and then kissed her again.

"I love you too," she replied just as a nurse walked into the room.

After being asked to step out so more nurses and Doctor Jacob could walk in, Desmond knew he had been given a second chance at happiness, and he wasn't going to waste it. He also knew the right people who could help him set up the perfect moment to make their relationship permanent.

Chapter Twenty-Four

Walking out of the bathroom wrapped in a towel. Kamala walked over to the mirror and slowly unfolded the towel. She looked intently at her face and body.

It had been two months since the attack and she never stopped being relieved that the bruises and swelling were gone. As she turned from side to side, she realized how far she had come since the incident with Dominic. She also had gotten to the point where she could think about him and not have an anxiety attack.

Since she awakened in the hospital, Desmond hadn't left her side. He made sure she had the best care from the doctors until she was released. She couldn't deal with going back to her home, because of the bad memories, so Desmond had insisted on her staying with him.

That was where she was at that moment, in their master bedroom that she loved since she first saw it. Being around Desmond, she felt safe and loved. Plus, he kept her mind off the craziness with Dominic who with the help of Tazmin and Demetria's legal connections, was found guilty of felony attempted murder, felony breaking and entering, and a list of other charges. Even though going through the high-profile trial was hard, she was able to cope with it because she had Desmond, his family, and Tazmin and her family to offer their support.

Most of all, her sisters were there and could understand from a female perspective what she was going through, and they even went with her to her counseling sessions.

She knew that her sisters felt responsible for what had happened to her, along with Kevin and Nicole. But after sitting down with each of them, she made them realize that the only person to blame was Dominic. He was paying for his bad judgement by losing his football career resulting in the League unexpectedly issuing a public apology to her.

He had lost his fortune when she won the civil suit against him. Then finally, he had lost his freedom, serving twenty-five years to life without the option of parole. When the sentence was read, Kamala felt as if a weight had been lifted off of her shoulders.

Closing her towel, Kamala looked over at the alarm clock and realized she had to hurry and get dressed, just as a pair of strong arms wrapped around her waist, bringing a smile to her face.

"Good morning beautiful," Desmond whispered before he kissed her bare shoulder causing her to lay her head back on his shoulder.

"It's better now that you are here," she replied smiling as he tightened his hold on her waist.

"That's good to hear! What's going through that pretty head of yours?" he asked as they both looked into the mirror at each other.

She inhaled deeply as she tried to commit that moment to memory, "Just thinking about everything that has happened and how grateful I am to have you and my family to support me," she replied as she turned in his arms.

"Baby, you mean so much to all of us and we want you to be happy. When everything happened, we were trying to stay strong for you," he stated before he kissed her and pulled back too soon for her liking earning a groan from her, which caused him to chuckle.

I'm just glad it's over, and we can move on with our lives," she replied as she pressed her body closer to him causing his eyes to ignite with desire as his hold on her tightened and she could feel his member respond to their closeness.

"Kamala, if you don't stop right now, we are going to be late to Tazmin's baby shower," he whispered as he started to kiss her neck causing her eyes to close as each kiss sent a shockwave to her womanhood.

Letting her towel fall to the floor, "I think we have plenty of time," she whispered before she brought his lips to hers.

As things started to heat up, Kamala knew that being with Desmond was where she belonged, and she was going to enjoy every mesmerizing moment.

Standing in the grand ballroom of the Peninsula Chicago, Kamala was dressed in her rose-colored dress. The dress had an effortless surplice style - a faux wrap caused by a diagonally crossed bodice that created a deep "V" neckline. Kamala loved the fluidity of the dress as it skimmed her curves before it elegantly cascaded down to the floor.

Looking around the room lavishly decorated with elegant place settings on each table complemented with fresh flowers. Most of all, she watched Tazmin, as she laughed and finally, she was able to enjoy herself after so much drama.

A smile lit up Kamala's face as she looked over at Desmond and Adonis as they held the babies and were making funny faces at them. Then she looked over at her other sisters as they sat with Adonis and Desmond's family laughing and cutting up as usual. It warmed her heart to see everyone she loved finally happy and enjoying life.

"What are you smiling about?" Tazmin asked as she stood beside Kamala and linked her arm through hers.

"I just realize how truly blessed I am to have all of you in my life," Kamala replied as she wiped a tear from her cheek.

"We all have been through a lot of shit, but you know what? We made it through it all in one piece, because we have each other and that will never change," Tazmin stated as she hugged Kamala.

Pulling apart, "I love you Sis," Kamala said as she wiped the tears from Tazmin's cheek.

Smiling and also wiping a tear from Kamala's cheek, "I love you too Sis," Tazmin replied. "Now, it's time for your surprise, godmother," Tazmin revealed as she smiled brightly causing Kamala to frown before she noticed Tazmin was looking behind her.

When she turned around, she gasped when she saw Desmond down on one knee with an open ring box that held a 3-carat white diamond cushion-cut engagement ring. The beads of diamonds that encircled the band winked as they rivaled in vain against the brilliant fire captured within the center stone. The beauty of the ring immediately brought tears to Kamala's eyes.

"Desmond!" she gasped as her heart rate started to race as he gently grabbed her left hand.

Looking up at her, he smiled while his eyes sought to convey what was in his heart.   "Kamala, I know this is long overdue because it seems as if I have loved you forever. And I realized that my life has been so much brighter with you in it. So," he paused and smiled, taking in her tear-filled face. "Will you do me the honor of becoming my wife?"

Covering her face as she attempted to stem the tears, she managed to nod her head repeatedly.

"Does that mean, yes?" he teased.

"Yes!" Kamala finally screamed before the room erupted into cheers as he slid the ring onto her shaky finger. When he stood up, pulling her into his arms, Kamala kissed him with all the love she had for the man who had shown her what true love felt like.

Epilogue

Eight months later, Kamala stood by the window in her orchid-colored top with the surplice bodice and a flattering empire waistline with black straight fitted Capri pants that she had paired with black wedged sandals.

Looking at Adonis and Tazmin as they held their sons on their laps as they posed for was the boys' first birthday party pictures, Kamala realized time had flown by when she least expected it. The boys were growing up so fast, and already trying to walk. Chuckling, Kamala remembered the shocked expression on Tazmin's face when she suggested that the boys were moving out of the way for another baby.

Hunter and Hayden were so cute with their vibrant gray eyes like their father, but they had Tazmin's stubborn attitude, which she completely denied. Watching their eyes light up as the waiters brought in their birthday cake decorated in different photos of the boys, Kamala's smile brightened. She loved them as she would her own kids, and she was determined to always be there for them.

She also couldn't help thinking about starting her family. Since their wedding two months before, she and Desmond had spent more time in their bed, than they had anywhere else in their penthouse. Thinking about Desmond, always caused her body to hum with need, and she couldn't imagine that reaction ever going away as her love for him grew each day.

Hearing a loud squeal brought her out of her thoughts, just as the boys each grabbed a handful of cake and shoved it into their little mouths. Everyone started laughing as the photographer continued to take pictures. Kamala laughed more as the boys tried to share with their parents and ended up smashing the cake into Tazmin and Adonis's face. Shaking her head as Demetria and Reyna came to their rescue and helped them all get cleaned up. Kamala knew that those boys were going to be a handful, but she was going to love every moment of it as they grew up into men.

Wiping her cheek when she felt a tear rolling down her face, Kamala frowned when she realized that she was so emotional.

"Baby, are you alright?" Desmond asked as he walked up to her and pulled her into his arms causing her to sigh.

Loving the feel of his arms around her, "I'm fine, just got a little weepy watching the boys," she whispered before she kissed him.

"You've been crying a lot lately; do we need to call your doctor?" he asked as he ran his hands down her back causing her to moan and him to chuckle.

"No, I'm fine! It's just my crazy prcgnancy hormones," she replied smiling before he froze, and then he looked down at her with a smile developing on his face.

"I'm going to be a dad?" he asked as he put his hand on her stomach.

Nodding her head, "Yes, you are in seven months," she replied before he started laughing as he picked her up causing her to squeal as she put her arms around his neck.

"God, I love you so much," he said as he lowered her back to the floor, and then kissed her.

"What's going on?" Kingsley asked as she was gently rocking her two-month-old son, Davis Josiah Lewis.

Looking around the room, Kamala realized they had gained the attention of everyone in the room. When she looked at Tazmin, who was the only person to know about her pregnancy, Tazmin had tears in her eyes as she smiled at Kamala.

"I just found out we're having a baby!" Desmond yelled causing everyone to cheer as they all came over and started hugging and congratulating them.

While hugging her family and friends, Kamala realized that producing music was their career, but she would be focusing more on producing love together with her handsome and loving husband.

About The Author

As a little girl, Leanora always had a notebook, where she could write her dreams and fantasies down. Growing into adulthood, she would read other authors work and say to herself that she wanted to do the same thing of being a published author.

At the age of 31, she decided to write her first novel titled *The Caress of a Younger Man*. Since then, she has followed it by *Heavenly Kingdom* and started The Voluptuously Curvy and Loving It Series, which focuses on plus-sized women and the men they love. Leanora started the series, because she wanted to create a movement for plus-sized women in the world, so that they could feel appreciated as beautiful and intelligent, who also deserve a happy ending.

In the Voluptuously Curvy and Loving It Series, the books are titled *Smooth As Silk, Finding Love Within, His Forgotten Lover, Drafted For Love*, and last but not least *Planning For Forever*. Recently, Leanora released a new series titled The Musical Curves Series which starts with *Rhymes from the Heart* and then *Producing Love Together*.

Throughout the entire process of becoming a published author, Leanora appreciates all the authors that were generous enough to offer their advice and knowledge.

Reading Group Guide

Let The Fun Begin!

1. Kamala had everything a person could ask for, she had a great career, money, owned a lovely home, and a group of loving friends, yet she still wasn't happy. What was the true cause of her unhappiness, and do you think she finally found it by the end of the book?

2. Desmond was living the high life as a successful music producer, dating gorgeous women. So why was Desmond still not satisfied with his life? Was he being greedy or was he just tired of loveless relationships?

3. Being an only child can be very lonely but meeting Tazmin and becoming a part of her family seemed to help Kamala's loneliness. How do you see Tazmin and Kamala's friendship? Is true sisterhood only achieved by being siblings or can two friends really become that close?

4. The characters in *Producing Love Together* all have busy lives, how do you feel about having a busy career and juggling a family? Do you think one would eventually interfere with the other?

5. When Dominic entered Kamala's life again, do you think she should have gone out with him, or waited and talked to Desmond first? Why?

6. When Kamala walked in on Desmond and Riley in the studio, was her reaction normal? How would you have handled the situation?

7. With the history that Dominic and Kamala shared, what do you think caused Dominic to finally snap when Kamala tried to end things?

8. Losing a parent is a challenging situation to handle, but for the Foster sisters, it was worse, because their parents were murdered, and they were the ones to find their bodies. With Tazmin being the oldest, she shouldered a lot of responsibility as she cared for her sisters. In that same situation, could you have done the same thing as Tazmin, or would you have done something different and why? Also, would visiting their graves yearly help you cope with their deaths and why?

9. Kamala's love for Desmond never diminished through all those years, even as he continued to date other women. Do you think she was crazy to keep waiting for him and why? Also is it true that you can't help who you love? Do you think it's possible to find true love and happiness and why?

10. After Kamala walked away from Desmond outside of the studio, Desmond received advice from Adonis and the other guys. Do you feel their advice was good advice to get Kamala back and why? Do you think Adonis was a good friend to help Desmond smooth things over with Tazmin and the other ladies when they showed up at Desmond's house and why? Also should the ladies help Desmond or stay out of it?

Connect with Author Leanora Moore at the info below!

Website:
www.leanoracowan.com

Facebook:
www.facebook.com/leanora moore78

Twitter:
@leanora_moore

Email:
Leanora.cowan@yahoo.com

Also, get ready for the next in this series!

Composing Her Desire:
Volume Three

Made in the USA
Columbia, SC
22 August 2022